THE FREELANCER TRILOGY

Traitor's Code
Prince's Mission
Assassin

TRAITOR'S CODE

FREELANCER 1

JANE KILLICK

Elly Books

Brother Andre lied. His monk's robes were a sham, his documentation was forged and the reason he had hired me was because he was running from the Fertillan Guard. Blinded by the money, I took his payment, accepted him on board my spaceship and asked no questions. That one mistake changed my life forever and ended the lives of many innocent people.

Brother Andre was one of a handful of passengers I had agreed to take to Serilla. The passenger run was supposed to be an easy stopgap between more challenging freelance jobs and, apart from the need to be polite to everyone all the time, that's exactly what it appeared to be. The only novelty about the entire journey was the presence of a real, live chicken which a young couple had brought with them to present as a gift at a family wedding. The only gift the bird gave to me was the acrid smell of chicken poo which hung like damp in my cargo hold.

On arrival at Serilla, I held my breath as I walked through the hold to the controls that would allow the passengers to disembark. I thumped down on the panel and listened for the sweet groaning of metal as the mechanism began to move. Chinks of light from Serilla pierced through the cracks that formed between the doors and I stood in the breeze drifting in from the moon colony. It blew a wisp of my long dark hair from my face and I breathed deeply to take away the cloying smell and reacquaint myself with the familiar tang of recycled air that had been re-breathed a thousand times by the overcrowded population.

Freddi, my one and only crew member, brought the passengers down to join me. He walked slowly, ambling with that lopsided walk he has, due to the accident which damaged his pelvis when he was an adolescent. It had stunted his growth a little, but it had not damaged his inner strength. What he had been through was enough for two lifetimes and the toll of his experience was etched into the lines of his face. Despite his suffering, he still had a full head of hair, even if more than half of its ginger strands had turned to grey.

He told the passengers to wait at a safe distance and I wrinkled my nose at him as he joined me at the controls.

"We're going to have to clean up in here when they're gone," I said to him quietly.

"When you say, 'we', do you actually mean 'me'?" said Freddi.

He frowned at me, but I saw he was smiling. Freddi and I had travelled in space together for a long time and he knew I did my fair share.

I glanced behind at the chicken which was staring out through the bars of a compact carrying case being held by the man from the wedding couple. Squatting down next to it, almost camouflaged against the dark in his black monk's robes, was Brother Andre. He seemed to be talking to the poor bird. Or maybe he was blessing it.

The doors fully opened to reveal the port of Serilla in all its ugly glory. Like most of the worlds in the Rim, the moon had no breathable atmosphere – in fact, it had no atmosphere at all – and so we had taxied the ship into a giant, enclosed, arrival hangar. Artificial lights blazed down onto the crowd of people milling about in front of us. There were crew attending to their vessels, officials in uniform checking documentation, traders and hustlers and probably pickpockets and criminals all jammed in together.

Through the centre of them all snaked a queue of arrivees waiting to pass through immigration. Freddi and I, being frequent travellers, paid a lot of money for a visa to bypass that indignity. Not the case for our hapless passengers.

With the ramp firmly extended, Freddi beckoned the passengers forward. Wide-eyed with anticipation, they filed out slowly. Only the chicken looked bewildered as it stared out from behind the door of its cage. A door which, I swear, looked as if it might be loose.

Brother Andre was the only one to stop and say goodbye. He clasped my hand between his palms and smiled. "It has been an honour, Captain Cassy," he said. "May blessings be upon you."

With that, he pulled up the hood of his robe and slipped discreetly into the crowd.

At that moment, a shriek rose from somewhere near the queue of new arrivals. Followed by a squawk and the sight of a very terrified chicken flapping its clipped wings as it made a doomed attempt to fly above the startled people below. It landed on the head of a woman who began screaming and waving her arms madly.

The chicken was knocked off its impromptu perch and fell somewhere behind her. More or less everyone in the whole place was shouting and pointing and panicking. The crowd jostled, a handful of chicken feathers flew into the air and came back down on them like confetti, while officials in uniform waded into the whole mess barking orders about remaining calm which were totally ignored.

"How the vac did that happen?" said Freddi.

"I'm not entirely sure," I said. "But before he left, I thought I saw Brother Andre doing something near the chicken's cage."

"The mild-mannered monk?"

I shrugged and continued to watch the chaos in front of us. Eventually, someone managed to grab hold of the bird and contain it. An official fired a blank warning shot into the air and the noise startled enough people to their senses to stop the panic.

"I better go out and track down some supplies," said Freddi. "We're getting low on… well, almost everything."

"See if you can get us another job while you're at it," I said. "Preferably one that doesn't involve chickens."

He laughed. "Aye aye to that."

I watched Freddi go and stepped back into the ship, only to realise I had left myself the unpleasant task of cleaning up the cargo hold. I sighed and tried to remember where I had put the cleaning materials.

But I never got to collect the cleaning materials.

The sound of boots marching onto my ship made me turn.

I was confronted by three men in the brown uniform of the Fertillan Guard. With the light of Serilla behind them, they formed three monolith silhouettes with the identical cut of their trousers, their jackets buttoned up to the neck and their peaked hats pulled down tight across their brows. The one in the middle stood a little in front of the other two and seemed to be in charge.

"Is this your vessel?" he demanded.

I felt the shiver of nerves go up my back. "It is."

"We have reason to believe you have been harbouring a fugitive."

"A fugitive? Don't be ridiculous!"

"We need to ask you some questions." He gestured to one of his subordinates who stepped forward to grab my arm.

"Hey!" I tugged my arm back, but it was held tightly in his grasp. "This is Serilla! You have no jurisdiction here."

But they didn't listen. I was dragged from the entrance and taken further inside.

I struggled and shouted and screamed at them, but my protestations were useless. There were three of them and only one of me: a hostage inside my own ship.

Chapter Two

The Fertillan Guard dragged me by the elbow so hard I felt my ligaments stretch as he marched through the corridors to the crew lounge. He flung me down onto the couch and my bottom landed hard on the lightly padded seat. I rubbed my arm where his thumb had dug into my flesh and felt where a bruise was starting to form.

He stood back, the depths of his eyes shadowed by the brim of his hat, and clasped his hands behind his back. He said nothing, but his whole demeanour suggested he was standing guard.

The one who had spoken to me on the ramp marched up behind him. "Thank you, Trevel," he said. Trevel merely nodded an acknowledgement.

"I am Marshal Commander Regellan," he said. Despite myself, I felt a ripple of trepidation run through me. Everyone on Fertilla knows who he is. He took off his hat and tucked it under his arm so I could see his face clearly for the first time.

I recognised him instantly. Marshal Commander Stephen Regellan, the head of the Fertillan Guard, better known as Prince Stephen Regellan, brother to King Richard of Fertilla. He had the wide Regellan nose that was a trademark of his family along with the dark brown hair and blue eyes he shared with his brothers.

"You have no right to come in here like this," I said. I was trying to be defiant, but I think my voice actually sounded a little scared.

Prince Stephen/Commander Regellan looked unruffled. In fact, he looked entirely comfortable in his position of power. I got the feeling that if he turned to Trevel and ordered him to shoot me, he would do it without a moment's hesitation.

"On the contrary," he said. "I have every right. You are a Fertillan citizen, this ship is registered in Fertilla, so we are effectively all on Fertillan territory."

I didn't doubt that it was true. Not as if I could do anything about it if it wasn't.

Stephen turned to Trevel. "Organise a thorough search of the ship."

"Yes, Sire." Trevel turned on his heel and went off to do his master's bidding.

I had horrible visions of my beloved ship being torn to pieces by Fertillan Guard thugs. "What is it you want?" I asked.

"We'll know when we find it," said Stephen.

I was not reassured. I searched his face to look for clues to his motive, but I saw nothing other than supreme confidence.

The soothing feminine voice of the ship came from the speakers above. "Crew information: six Fertillan Guards have entered through the bay and are making their way deeper inside."

I know she's just a computer and her artificial intelligence doesn't include the ability to have emotions, but I thought she sounded a little afraid.

Stephen glanced up at the ceiling. Everyone does that, it's a common human reaction, even though they know the computer isn't actually based inside the speakers. "They are here on my orders," he said. "If you check the documents filed with your systems, you will see the search is all in order."

"But Cassy," said the ship. "They have entered your personal room."

"It's okay, Ship," I told her. "We have to let them."

"If you say so, Cassy." And she fell silent again.

Stephen raised an eyebrow. "You call your ship, 'Ship'?"

"We never got around to thinking of another name," I said. Anyway, we decided it suited her.

Stephen reached into his pocket, pulled out a personal tablet and showed it to me. "We're looking for this man."

I peered at his P-tab. On the screen was a picture of Brother Andre, except he was not dressed in monk's robes, but in civilian dress. Rather fine and expensive civilian dress at that.

I shrugged. "Who is he?"

"Andrus Hoggard. We have reason to believe he bought passage on this vessel."

I shook my head while the neurons in my brain were firing, trying to work out what the vac was going on. "We brought four passengers from Fertilla and none of them went by that name. You can check the manifest."

"I assure you, we have already done so. Falsifying a ship's manifest is a criminal offence."

"Which is why I wouldn't be stupid enough to do it," I said.

"Hmm." He turned away from me as if bored with the conversation and consulted his P-tab.

It gave me a moment to think.

The whole thing with the chicken suddenly made sense. Brother Andre/Andrus Hoggard had tampered with the chicken's cage just before departure so it would escape and cause mayhem. Presumably so he could slip away in all the chaos.

I had transported a wanted man on forged documentation and now I was in the drakh.

Half an hour later, I still hadn't come up with a plan to get myself out of it when I heard a commotion in the corridor. As it got closer, I recognised Freddi's complaining voice.

"Get off me!" he was saying. "I can walk perfectly well without your help, you know!"

Trevel appeared at the entrance to the crew lounge holding Freddi by the elbow like he had held me. Except that Freddi, being somewhat shorter, was being hoiked up by his arm so his feet were barely touching the ground.

"Sire," announced Trevel to Stephen. "I found this individual boarding the ship."

"That's because I work here," said Freddi. He struggled in Trevel's grip, but his arm was held tight and it did him no good. "I'm allowed to walk back onto my own ship, aren't I?"

Stephen looked at Freddi with disinterest. "Fine. Put him with the other one."

By 'the other one', he evidently meant me. Trevel thrust Freddi forward and he stumbled on his bad leg until he was able to recover and compose himself. He yanked down his crumpled shirt and came and sat next to me.

"What's going on, Cassy?" he said.

"Don't know." If I had been able to speak without the Fertillan Guard hearing, I would have said more.

Freddi stared at Stephen until a look of realisation formed on his face. He whispered: "Isn't that…?"

I nodded.

"What the vac is he doing here?"

Stephen turned, even though the question wasn't directed at him, and showed Freddi the picture on his P-tab. "We're looking for this man," he said.

Another look of recognition passed across Freddi's face. "Brother Andre?" he said. "What do you want with him?"

My guts clenched. He'd just thrown away our deniability card.

"We want very much to find him," said Stephen.

"Well, he's not here. He left with the other passengers."

I kicked Freddi on the ankle.

"What?" he said.

I gave him a hard stare.

Stephen ignored me and focussed all of his attention on Freddi. "Where was he going?"

"He didn't say," said Freddi. "Other than he was on a pilgrimage. He went wherever monks go when they're on a pilgrimage, I suppose. I don't know, he didn't talk much. He spent most of his time praying."

"Hmm," said Stephen. He walked away again and spoke to a member of the Fertillan Guard who I could just about see was standing in the corridor.

Freddi turned to me and mouthed the word, *sorry*.

It probably didn't matter in the grand scheme of things. They clearly knew more about the man – the fugitive? – than I did.

We were made to sit silently on the couch for several hours while members of the Fertillan Guard crawled all over my ship. I wondered what the drakh they were looking for, as surely they knew that Andre/Hoggard had disembarked. Stephen stayed in the crew lounge with us, but asked no more questions. He paced the room, consulted the screen of his P-tab and occasionally went into the corridor to speak on his communicator. I couldn't hear what he was saying, but I could see there was also an armed guard out there ready to shoot us if we tried to make a run for it.

Perhaps we were being kept there before being arrested and taken to some Deity-abandoned jail cell. I began to think that making a run for it might not be a bad option.

Not long after that, Trevel returned. "Sire," he said.

Stephen looked up from his screen. "Have you completed the search?"

"Yes, Sire."

"Good."

"But there's something else." The subordinate took a step back to suggest he wanted a private word. Stephen followed him out into the corridor.

"Do you think they've found something?" said Freddi.

"I don't know."

"What the vac could they have been looking for?"

"Shh!" I kicked Freddi in the ankle again as I strained to hear what the two men were saying. Whatever it was, they were too far away for us to hear. Stephen didn't look best pleased.

The pair marched back in.

Trevel hung back by the door while Stephen looked at us with suspicion. "Well," he said. "It seems you have friends in high places, Individual Sesaan Cassandra." He looked down at something on his P-tab and frowned. "So, for the time being, I will let you go."

I tried to look smug even though the rush of relief was running through my body.

"But don't try to leave Serilla. It will take a while for clearance to go through for your ship."

He turned on his heel, looking somewhat annoyed, and barked at Trevel to follow him.

"Friends in high places?" asked Freddi when they had gone.

I shrugged.

"I thought you only had friends in low places."

"I thought so too," I said.

Chapter Three

I STOOD AT THE entrance to my room and I could have almost cried.

If Freddi hadn't been there, I think I might have.

It was beyond a mess. The Fertillan Guard hadn't just come in and gone through my personal drawers and pulled out my personal stuff, they had taken my clothes and flung them all over the place. They hadn't just searched the bed, they had dismantled it and left the component parts in a pile in the middle of the floor. They hadn't just searched the room, they had taken knives to the walls and cut holes to reveal the wiring and pipework inside.

"Bastards," said Freddi.

"Yeah," I said. There were no words.

"They did the same thing to mine. The Deity knows what they did to the rest of the ship."

"Are you there, Ship?" I asked.

"Yes, Cassy," she replied from above.

"Are you are okay?"

"I am fully functional, Cassy."

"They didn't hurt you?" I asked.

"Only living things feel pain, Cassy."

"Yes, Ship," I said.

Freddi touched me gently on the arm. "Come on, let's numb the pain at one of the local bars."

"I dunno, Freddi. I should make a start clearing up."

"Don't worry about that now. It'll still be here when you come back."

"That's what I'm worried about."

"You'll worry less after a couple of drinks. I'll pay if you like."

So I let him take me to the bar. I didn't have the strength to argue.

THE BAR THAT Freddi found was, like most of the city, cut directly into the rock of the moon.

In humanity's glory days, they say people lived out on the surface of planets under blue skies with breathable air. But when the Oblivion War made the centre of the galaxy uninhabitable and prevented us from travelling beyond its outer edge, people were left to survive the best they could. That meant burrowing underground to create habitats which could be filled with heat and air, or building giant city-size enclosures on the surface of the few worlds that we were able to colonise.

We called the part of the galaxy, between the destroyed centre and the outer barrier, the 'Obsidian Rim', because the few stars that existed in that narrow region of space made the blackness around us seem even darker.

Freddi led me into the interior of the moon through a series of tunnels which opened out into a central communal area. From there, we passed through a modest door into a circular bar with a serving area in the middle and seating around the edges. Most of the sections were full, as it was evening local time, but I managed to find a cubbyhole with a couple of comfortable seats and a table to sit and wait for Freddi to get the drinks he had offered to pay for.

My beer arrived in a straight glass that was full to the brim and spilled a little as Freddi put it on the table. I leant forward and sipped without risking lifting it to my lips. The subtle sweet taste touched my tongue and almost immediately released its bitter tones as I swallowed and waited for the alcohol to dull my brain.

Freddi was complaining about the size of the bar bill, and saying he had been overcharged for being an off-worlder, but I didn't pay any attention. The trauma of the day was still with me.

I interrupted him – I had made a decision and it couldn't wait for him to finish blathering. "We leave right away," I said. "As soon as the ship is cleared for take-off."

"And we've got supplies on board," Freddi added. "Plus, hopefully, another job."

"Even if we haven't. I don't want to stay here a moment longer than we have to. We've got some money stashed away, we can take the ship to Nanci, she'll do us a good price on repairs."

"It's only cosmetic damage. It can wait."

"You might be able to sleep soundly with violent slashes in your wall, but I can't."

"You haven't been stranded in unoccupied space with no qubition, and food running out. By the Deity, that's when you have trouble sleeping."

I suspected this was an allusion to Freddi's former life as a pirate. He rarely mentioned it, but on the occasions he did, I had the feeling his experiences were pretty horrific.

"What do you think the Fertillan Guard were looking for?" he said.

"Who cares?" I downed a mouthful of beer. It wasn't very strong and the neurons in my brain were still firing too energetically.

Freddi pulled his P-tab from his pocket. "What was Brother Andre's real name again?"

"Don't look him up," I said.

"Don't you want to know who he is?"

"Not really. He lied to us. He fooled us. Forget about it and drink your beer."

Freddi's beer remained untouched in front of him. "I keep thinking about the way he blessed you before he left the ship – it was almost as if he was saying sorry. A bit unusual for the average criminal."

"The average criminal doesn't have Prince Stephen Regellan chasing after him."

"Exactly!" said Freddi.

I had inadvertently spurred him on to be even more curious and he ran a search on his P-tab.

"Here we are," he said. I saw he had found exactly the same picture that Stephen had showed us. "Andrus Hoggard: staff at the royal household of Fertilla. That's all it says."

The rest was probably classified, I thought. "Now you've

satisfied your curiosity, are you going to drink your beer or what?"

Freddi put his P-tab away and, at last, started to join me on the road to inebriation.

While we'd been talking, a child of about eight years old had run into the bar and was causing commotion by going from table to table. He – because I realised, after a moment, it was a boy – looked like one of the local working-class kids. His hair was short, but unkempt and his clothes looked worn as if they were the only set he had, or were hand-me-downs from another kid who had grown out of them.

He came to our table; running so fast that he didn't quite stop in time and nudged my drinking arm so I almost spilled my beer. "Oi!"

His wide eyes looked terrified.

"Cassy?" he asked.

I jolted at hearing my name. I had no idea who the boy was and, I swear, I had never seen him before. "Go away."

"You're Cassy, aren't you?"

I looked across at Freddi. His expression showed he was as clueless as me.

"What do you want?" I asked the boy.

"You have to come." He grabbed my arm and pulled. This time he really did spill my beer.

"Hey!" I wrenched my arm back again.

"You have to come, *please*," he begged. "Brother Andre needs you."

I went as cold as the beer I was drinking. "Well, I don't need him."

Freddi raised an eyebrow. "Aren't you curious?"

"No," I said.

"You need to come *now*!" said the boy.

I don't know if Freddi's curiosity had infected me or the beer had started to numb my sense of judgement, but somehow I allowed the boy to pull me from my seat and out of the bar.

He encouraged us to follow him as he ran around the edge of the communal centre and down a side alley, looking behind every now and then to check we were following. The boy was fast and nimble and not easy to keep up with. I heard Freddi complain about the pain in his hip as he slipped further behind.

The boy took us to a run-down residential sector which, by the look of some of the people standing on its streets, was popular with sex workers. There was even the smell of sex in the air.

None of this fazed the boy at all as he weaved his way through to a small hut-like dwelling and went inside. I glanced back to make sure Freddi was still heading in the right direction, and followed the boy.

Stale air hung in the one room which was lit by the soft glow of a single lamp in the corner, just enough to reveal the objects of somebody's simple life. There was a table, a small stove, a cupboard and one wall adorned with a woven mat to disguise the grubby surface behind. A young woman knelt at the end of a mattress placed at the far end. In front of her, lying flat on his front, was the figure of a man dressed in black monk's robes. The hilt of a knife stuck up from the middle of his back.

"Are you Cassy?" said the woman.

I couldn't answer. I was staring at the body on the mattress and realising, as my eyes got used to the dim light, that it was Brother Andre. He was alive, but his breathing was laboured and his robes were soaked in the blood oozing from the knife wound.

"He's been asking for you," she said.

She stood and reached out her hand for the boy. He curled his fingers around hers and she took him out into the street, almost bumping into Freddi in their rush to get away.

Freddi stopped in the doorway. "By the Deity!" he said.

"Cass–" gasped Brother Andre. Or Andrus Hoggard, or whatever his name was.

I knelt at the side of the mattress. "What did you call *me* for?" I said in desperation. "You need a doctor!" I looked at the knife in his back and knew that, from where it was sticking out, it had probably punctured a lung, if not other organs. In a rash moment, I thought about pulling it out, but then realised this would almost certainly cause him to bleed to death. If he wasn't bleeding to death already.

"It's important," he said.

"What?" I bent down so my ear was closer to his mouth.

"*Important*," he said again. He let out a feeble cough and spat blood onto the mattress.

He reached out a deathly white hand and held onto my sleeve with surprising strength. "You must…" He drew a rasping breath. "…must deliver the code."

"What code? You're not making sense."

He lifted his head from the mattress.

"Lie still, you've been badly injured."

He ignored my pleas and so I took the weight of his head and laid it on my lap. There was a coldness about his skin that told me life had almost left his body.

"Our salvation," he said. "Our salv–"

The word died on his final breath.

His damaged lungs expelled the last of the air inside them with a hollow sigh.

"No!" I pushed his head from my lap and tried to turn over the body to resuscitate him, but the knife sticking out of his ribcage got in the way and his body rolled onto its front again.

"Cassy, we need to get out of here," called Freddi from the doorway.

"We can't leave him!"

"He's dead, Cassy."

Freddi lurched forward as he was pushed from behind. He stumbled on his bad leg, but reached out for the wall and stopped himself from falling.

We both looked back to see the monolith silhouette of a man dressed in Fertillan Guard uniform standing in the doorway.

As he stepped inside, the dull light from the lamp fell across his face and revealed it was Trevel.

Chapter Four

I was arrested on suspicion of murder and taken to a jail cell on the Fertillan Guard ship. I didn't see what happened to Freddi – we got separated – but I presumed his fate was the same as mine and he was sitting in a cell not far from me.

I was confined in a square box of grey metal walls barely wider than I was tall. I sat on the narrow bench along the back and stared at the door without a handle. It could have been almost any jail cell on any world.

At some point, I had run my hand through my hair and caused Andre's blood to become smeared onto the strands where it had dried and made them stick together. There was blood on my shirt, on my trousers and encrusted into the lines of my hands, so everywhere I looked that wasn't a grey wall reminded me of his death.

I jolted at the sound of the unbolting of the lock and caught a glimpse of the whiteness of the corridor before the doorway was filled with the brown silhouette of a man in Fertillan Guard uniform.

He stepped inside and someone closed the door behind him.

The blue eyes of Prince Stephen Regellan looked down on me with royal superiority. "Individual Sesaan Cassandra," he said, articulating every syllable of my full name like it gave him some power over me. "Your protected status won't be enough to get you off this time."

"I didn't kill him," I said, deciding not to admit I didn't know what 'protected status' was or who had protected me.

"You were caught, literally, red-handed."

I rubbed my right thumb across my left palm and some of Andre's dried blood flaked off. "I didn't kill him," I said. "I tried to save him."

He stared at me with his blue eyes. It was like they were burrowing into my mind.

"Look," I said, "if I'd wanted him dead, I would have done it while he was asleep on board my ship and thrown him out an airlock. Only a stupid person would commit murder in a crowded place like Serilla."

"Let's imagine for a moment that you are not stupid," said Stephen.

He paused, letting his words settle in the room, as if they might give me some hope.

"Why did you take him to a prostitute?" he said.

"She was a prostitute?"

"It appears so."

"I didn't take him."

"Yet you knew he was there."

"I had no idea where he was. I didn't even want to see the lying drakh-ball again after you lot trashed my ship. A boy found me and took me to him. You can ask in the bar if you don't believe me."

I could see by the way he was frowning that he didn't believe a word of it. "Bit unusual, isn't it? For a man dressed as a monk to go to the sex quarter."

"Prostitutes don't just take money for sex," I said. "Some will take money for other services. At least, that's been my experience."

"Your experience?" asked Stephen.

"I'm a freelancer with a ship. Sex parties in space pay well, especially for the wealthy who live on the more prudent parts of the Rim. I make it my business to talk to the sex workers to ensure they get their fair share of the money. When you get to know them, they have some very interesting stories to tell."

"You think Hoggard paid the prostitute to hide him?"

I shrugged. "Maybe pretending to be a monk left him sexually frustrated and he paid her for her usual services. I don't know. You better ask her."

Stephen smiled. "Oh, we will."

I realised if she had taken money to hide him from the Fertillan Guard, I had just dropped her right in it. I felt my face flush with shame.

"This is all very interesting, Individual Cassandra, but it doesn't explain why you were there."

"The boy came and got me."

"So you said. A bit unusual for a dying man, don't you think, not to call a medic or priest?"

"I wish he had found a medic or a priest, believe me." Sitting in the stark metal cell, I wished he had found anyone but me. "I can only assume the boy saw my name on his travel documents or something."

"Or maybe he wanted to give you something or tell you something."

"He didn't."

"Then I ask again, why were you there?"

I side-stepped his question. "I don't know why the boy dragged me there, I swear. Hoggard was almost dead by the time I arrived. I tried to save him, but he didn't regain consciousness."

It was only a half-lie. His dying words meant nothing to me.

"How convenient for you," said Stephen.

"Not really. Because if he'd given me something I could hand it over to you and get out of here."

Stephen turned abruptly, as if he had heard enough. He knocked on the inside of the cell door. It was opened by someone on the other side and I saw the white of the corridor again.

Stephen paused in the doorway. "I shall investigate your story, Individual Cassandra. In the meantime, you might want to consider if you need to change it."

He stepped into the white and the door slammed shut behind him with a clang of metal which reverberated around the cell and through the bench I was sitting on.

"Drakh."

Chapter Five

CHECKING OUT MY story apparently involved subjecting me to a strip search.

They made me take off my clothes and watched while I did so.

I shivered with the cold of indignity as I dropped my bloodied trousers, shirt and underwear on the floor.

I stood naked and exposed in my metal box while a woman – at least it was a woman – checked me intimately. By the time she got to raking through my hair and checking my armpits, my humiliation was complete.

I was given easy-recycle clothes to wear and locked back up again.

I MUST HAVE slept because I didn't hear the cell door open. I was only aware that someone else had entered my metal box.

I pulled myself up from my position lying on the bench with the sound of my easy-recycle clothes scrunching as I moved.

It was Prince Stephen again. Whatever the fake monk had done, it had to be personal for him to take such an interest.

"You're free to go," he said.

"What?" I was still sleepy.

"Your story checked out. There were dozens of witnesses in the bar, so we have no cause to hold you on suspicion of murder."

"That's it?"

"Unless you want to confess to a different crime," he said.

"No!"

A woman in Fertillan Guard uniform entered the cell carrying my clothes. It was the same woman who had examined me. She dumped them at my feet. "Get dressed."

I relieved myself of the unpleasant, scrunchy clothes they had given me and put my own back on. They were sweaty, smelly and encrusted with blood, but at least it was my sweat, my smell and someone else's blood.

Stephen didn't stay to watch. I thought he had gone, but when the woman led me out into the corridor I found that he was waiting.

Which was good because I realised, like a self-absorbed idiot, I had forgotten about Freddi.

"What about my shipmate?" I said.

"I can release Individual Frederus Aaron if you tell me something."

I felt the terror in my stomach: he wasn't going to let me go at all, this was a ruse to give me false hope and make me talk. "Brother Andre – I mean, Hoggard – didn't give me anything, he didn't tell me anything."

"That wasn't what I was going to ask," said Stephen.

"Oh." My brain tried to anticipate what he wanted so I had a nanosecond to prepare an answer, but I had no idea and it was like grasping air.

"Why did my father put you on a protected list?" said Stephen.

"Your father?" *Did he mean King John? King John was dead.*

"Yes, my father." He seemed absolutely serious.

"I never met King John," I said. "I mean, he died when I was a child."

"When I was a child too," said Stephen.

I saw the man inside the uniform at that moment. The man who had grown up without a father and must always have had that part of his life missing. He looked past me, deep in thought. "Curious."

"Yes." I half thought maybe my name had got muddled up with someone else and I shouldn't be on the list at all, but I didn't want to jeopardise my release and kept the theory to myself. "You will release me and Freddi?"

"Indeed." He seemed to return his thoughts to the present. He gestured to the woman. "Do all the necessaries, would you, Sergeant?"

"Yes, Sire."

He marched off down the corridor without so much as a glance back.

But he was true to his word. After signing a few things, I was reunited with Freddi and we walked free.

Chapter Six

"Too easy," said Freddi, shovelling a mouthful of the brown sludge he had just cooked into his mouth. He called it stew, but it was more like mush as whatever was in it had been cooked for so long it had lost its identity. Not that it tasted that bad. After many hours in a Fertillan cell, I was damned hungry.

I'd had a wash and a change of clothes and was starting to feel more human. The sense of vulnerability from my incarceration hadn't entirely left me, but I felt safer being in my own crew lounge on my own ship.

"What was easy?" I said.

"Getting out of there," said Freddi.

"Didn't feel easy to me." The memory of the woman's gloved hand probing intimate parts of my body was too fresh.

"Marshal Commander Prince Stephen Regellan personally questions us then lets us go?"

"He had no reason to keep us. We've done nothing wrong."

Freddi gave me a sideways glance across the table like I was being naive.

"Look, you said Hoggard worked for the royal household. I imagine whatever he did, it severely drakhed off the prince."

"Probably."

"It doesn't matter anyway," I said. "As soon as we get clearance to leave Serilla, we'll get the vac off this rock and put the whole thing behind us."

"Aye aye, Captain."

There was something about his tone which suggested he didn't entirely agree. "It's not an order, Freddi. But I don't want to stick around here, do you?"

"They let us go too easy, that's all I'm saying."

Fed up with the circular conversation, I stood up from the table. I picked up my bowl and glanced across to where Freddi had nearly scraped his clean. "Have you finished with that?"

"Almost." He ran his index finger around the inside to scoop up the very last vestiges of stew and stuck it in his mouth.

"Freddi, you're disgusting."

"Thank you," he said.

I picked up his bowl, but I didn't leave the table.

He looked up. "What?"

I took a deep breath. "There's, um, something I didn't tell you."

"What?" he said again.

"Hoggard said something to me before he died."

"He *what*?"

"He said 'deliver the code.'"

"What does that mean?"

"I don't know. He said it was our salvation."

"What does *that* mean?"

"I don't know! Probably nothing. I expect he was delirious, he'd lost a lot of blood."

"Why didn't you tell me this before?"

"I got arrested and thrown in a jail cell, it was kind of difficult."

"By the Deity, Cassy!"

I clutched the bowls closer to my body. Not that they were any comfort. "And there's something else…" I said.

His stare hardened.

"I didn't tell the prince. I told him Hoggard was already unconscious when I got there."

"You *lied* to the Marshal Commander of the Fertillan Guard?"

"It was only a little lie."

"By the Deity, Cassy!"

His disappointment in me filled the silence in the room. Strictly speaking, he was my employee and I was his captain and I didn't have to explain anything to him. But, in reality, he was my friend. Shipmates who don't work together when they travel in space often end up dead.

Ship broke the tense atmosphere with her soothing voice. "I thought you would like to know that the Serillan authorities have approved our documentation. We are cleared to leave."

Freddi stood up. "I'll ready the ship for take-off and plot a course to take us to Nanci for repairs," he said.

"No," I said. "Nanci's too close to Fertilla and I'd rather not enter Fertillan space if we don't have to. Take us into space and fire up the drive so we can wormhole as far away as possible."

"You want to burn expensive qubition without a freelance job to pay for it?"

"By the Deity, yes," I said.

Freddi nodded. "Aye aye, Captain."

And this time, I could see he was in full agreement.

<h1 style="text-align:center">CHAPTER SEVEN</h1>

RETURNED TO MY room to clear up the mess the Fertillan Guard had left.

It looked worse than I remembered. I tried to console myself that it was only 'stuff', that slashed walls could be mended and my strewn possessions could be put back in their place.

I wasn't very convincing.

Just as my body had been violated in the jail cell, I felt something of myself had been violated in that room. It was my sanctuary from everything. Whatever is going on in my life, whatever difficult freelance mission I have accepted, whatever mood Freddi is in, I can always escape to the one room which is truly mine and where I can be myself.

Except it didn't feel the same after it had been invaded.

"Oh, Ship," I said. "Tell me everything can be repaired."

"I suffered no serious damage, Cassy," said Ship. "Only cosmetic repairs are needed."

"Thank you, Ship."

I took a deep breath and mentally tried to block out the image of the room as a whole to concentrate on tidying one small bit at a time. I began by picking up my clothes, smoothing out the creases as best I could and putting them away.

"Cassy?" said Ship as I worked.

"Yes, Ship?"

"I love you, Cassy."

I stopped mid-way through folding a T-shirt. It was a strange thing for her to say. "Well, I love you too, Ship."

AFTER I HAD put away my clothes and sorted my bed, I decided I had had enough of clearing up the mess left by Fertillan Guard scum and I headed for the control room.

Although I can monitor the status of the ship, and even make adjustments to things such as our course and speed from almost any console, the equipment is more sophisticated in the control room. It's a large space for just me and Freddi. There are actually five consoles designed for a full crew, but we generally manage with no more than the two of us. On the few occasions I've taken on a job which required more hands on deck and hired more staff, it has been more trouble than it was worth.

The vandals had also rampaged through the control room. I had imagined there would be nothing for them to mess up as all the consoles and equipment are fixed in place. But they had gone up to every single one and removed the inspection panels which they left strewn across the floor. The Fertillan Guard had definitely been looking for something. It had to have been something small which could fit inside the base of a console which was already full of wiring and computer hardware. Whatever it was, I wouldn't be surprised if it had been stolen from the Regellan royal household, and whoever had killed Hoggard had done so to steal it from him.

My thoughts triggered the memory of Hoggard spitting blood as I knelt beside his dying body. I shook my head to push the memory away.

I picked up the panel nearest to me and leant it back against the base of the console. At least, I noticed, it had been unscrewed rather than wrenched or cut away from its position, so it would be relatively easy to put back again. But to do them all would be a long and laborious job which I was in no mood to tackle. I tiptoed over the other panels and made my way to the centre of the control room and the largest console. It was the captain's console which, naturally, was mine.

I saw Freddi had already set a course for deep space away from Serilla. It wouldn't be long before we were at a safe enough distance to operate the Quantum Entanglement Drive.

"Ship, where's Freddi?"

"He's in his room, Cassy," she replied.

I touched one of the two screens in front of me and opened communications. "Freddi, have you sorted out where we're going yet?"

"Oh, hi, Cassy," he said. I heard the crash of something falling over at the other end as I caught him by surprise. "Drakh!"

That's the problem with internal voice-only communications, they can catch you doing the most intimate of things unless you remember to put the system on 'do not disturb'. On this occasion, it sounded like Freddi had probably just knocked something over.

"I said, have you figured out where we're going yet?"

"Yeah, I've been doing the calculations," Freddi said. "I'm thinking the spaceport in the Riel system. It's far enough, but not too far and there's a lot of comings and goings for us to pick up work."

"Sounds good. Come up to the control room and let's get going."

"Righty-ho!" he said.

I closed the communication.

I looked up the Riel system and reminded myself of what it was like. It was a long time since I'd visited, but I had a few contacts there. It was a good choice.

"Cassy?" said Ship.

"Yes, Ship?"

"Your hair looks especially beautiful today."

It was an odd thing for her to say. I self-consciously brushed my hand lightly over the long dark strands of my hair. I have a feminine pride in my hair, which is why I keep it long when it would be much more practical to cut it short. Although I'd done nothing different to it when I washed it after getting out of jail.

"Thank you, Ship."

"It's the way the light hits it at a certain angle and reveals its auburn tones," said Ship.

That was more than odd. It was almost creepy. "Ship, are you feeling all right?"

"I don't have feelings, you know that, Cassy."

I dismissed it and pulled up the details Freddi had sent me about the journey to Riel. He'd already instructed the stellarship navigator to find a potential wormhole and estimate the amount of qubition to initiate a q-burst. We had enough to get us there with a little to spare, but we would be low on resources without more paying work, especially if we had to spend some of our money on repairs.

My worries about money – an occupational hazard for a free-lancer – were interrupted by Ship's soothing voice again. "I love the sparkle in your eyes when you look up to the ceiling to talk to me, Cassy. They are of the most beautiful brown."

I stopped reading the information on my screen, but I didn't look up to speak to her; unnerved that she might be looking into my eyes.

I was somewhat relieved when Freddi entered the control room.

He, like me, stepped over the panels to get to his preferred station, the one to the right of the captain's console. He pulled up our flight path on the single screen in front of him. "Almost there," he said. "Only a few more calculations when we make full stop and we'll be wormholing out of here."

"Good," I said.

"You don't sound too sure."

"I am, it's just… have you been talking with the ship recently?"

"I've had a few short conversations," he said. "Why?"

"Has she said anything… *weird* to you?"

"Weird? No." He thought about it for a second. "Well, she said that she loved me."

"That's weird," I pointed out.

"Not really," said Freddi. "I'm a very loveable person."

Ship interrupted. "We are approaching the set deep space

position," she said in her usual matter-of-fact way. "Readying for full stop."

Freddi and I watched the screens as they detailed the reverse thrust of the engines to slow us down and the manoeuvring into the position that Freddi had programmed. Beneath my feet, I felt the change in vibrations as the engines made their adjustments until, eventually, there were no vibrations at all. We had reached full stop.

"Making final calculations," Freddi said.

I waited and watched the screen as numbers that I didn't fully understand scrolled across it. I trusted Freddi and the ship to know what they were doing.

"Searching for potential wormholes," he said. "Okay… I think we have a winner."

My screen showed the animated pattern of a wormhole opening near our position and emerging close to the Riel system. More numbers indicated the exact amount of qubition for the necessary q-burst to make the journey. Then the numbers stopped changing. We were ready to go.

"Let's do it," I said.

Freddi executed the relevant commands on his screen and I waited for the familiar sound of a q-burst. It was like the rumble of thunder on a planet with atmosphere. One that seemed to surround you and be inside of you at the same time, that seemed to jolt your whole body forward while it remained standing still. It was the magic of the Quantum Entanglement Drive and the power of the qubition that made you feel, just for that moment, more than human. You were no longer an insignificant being living at the mercy of the Obsidian Rim, you were its master: bending space to travel outside of the normal rules of spacetime.

It is the thrill of the spacefarer. Once tasted, never forgotten, and always longed for.

I waited.

But I felt nothing.

I heard nothing.

I saw Freddi's puzzled face.

"What's going on?" I asked.

"I don't know."

His fingertips expertly tapped across the screen in front of him. "The QED hasn't fired."

"Why not?"

He shrugged.

"Ship?"

"Yes, Cassy?"

"What's up with the QED?"

"It's not working, Cassy."

"I figured that much out. *Why* isn't it working?"

"I don't know, Cassy."

I looked across to Freddi. "This is not right, she said the Fertillan Guards didn't do any substantial damage."

He shrugged again. "It doesn't make any sense. I checked all the systems myself. As far as I can tell, it should be working."

Ship spoke again. "I'm sorry, Cassy. I'm sorry, Freddi. If I could help you, you know I would. Because I love you both, you know that, don't you?"

Freddi raised his eyebrows and I could see he knew it wasn't only the QED that had problems. Something was up with the ship's operating system.

"Options?" I asked him.

"We have enough fuel to go back to Serilla," said Freddi. "But not enough to come back out here and try the QED again and then make it to Riel from wherever the wormhole spits us out. We could try buying some more fuel at Serilla, but…"

"We need a dedicated spaceport for that, really."

"Right. The other option is to stay here and see if I can fix it."

"Doesn't sound like we have much of a choice."

"Not really," he said. "I'll get started on figuring it out – assuming I *can* figure it out. Until then, we're stuck here."

Chapter Eight

I WAS WOKEN UP by the rumbling of our engines at full pelt and the frantic sound of Freddi's voice over the communicator. "Cassy! For the love of the Deity, will you answer me!"

I opened my eyes to the darkness of the night-time circuit in my room. "Freddi?"

"At last!"

"What's going on?"

"Pirates."

The word sent a shock of dread running through my body. Everyone who travels the Rim knows the best thing to do about pirates is to stay well clear of them.

I stumbled out of bed and reached for my clothes. My toe struck something hard on the floor which I hadn't got around to clearing up yet. I swore.

"Lights!" Brightness flooded the room and damn near blinded me. But it was enough for me to find the drawer where I kept my

Energy Expenditure handgun and my holster.

"Freddi, where are you?" I called out, as I made it to the door and hit the control.

"I'm outside your–" The door opened. "–room."

Freddi stood in front of me. There was a sheen of sweat on his face and the slight tremble of nervous energy to his body.

I strapped my gun's holster around my hips and secured the strap around my leg. "What's going on?"

"They saw us at full stop and tried to board, but the ship refused them permission to dock. I'm trying to outrun them, but their engines are at least as good as ours and we're almost out of fuel."

"We'll be stranded."

"And easy pickings."

We looked at each other; both knowing what that could mean.

"There's something else I can try, but we haven't got long," he said. "We need to get to the control room."

He ran up the corridor as best he could and I followed, pushing the mat of my unbrushed hair from my face as I shook off the last vestiges of sleep.

Freddi went straight to his console. "To do this, we're going to have to stop. If I cut the engines, they'll catch up with us. Do I have your permission, Captain?"

"Always," I said.

The rumble abruptly ceased as Freddi cut the power to the engines. I looked down at my own screen and saw we were drifting.

A clang of metal striking metal reverberated around the ship.

"What was that?" I said.

Ship answered. "Something has attached itself to my side."

"They're attaching mines to blast their way in," said Freddi.

"They really don't waste time, do they?"

"Freddi, you said there was something you could try."

He turned to me and took a deep breath. "I think I've fixed the QED enough to fire off a small q-burst."

"So we can wormhole out?"

"No, but it might be enough to scare off the pirates and kill off a few of them at the same time."

"Isn't that dangerous?" I said.

"That's why I wanted to ask you first."

Messing about with qubition, especially when it comes to causing explosions was what got the human race in the mess that we're in. If it wasn't for the qubition-powered bombs, there would have been no Oblivion War.

"I don't know, Freddi."

"I've been preparing for a possible pirate attack ever since I joined the ship. I've run the calculations a million times, it's just with the QED playing up, I can't be one hundred per cent certain it's going to do what I think it's going to do."

Another clang reverberated around the ship. "Do it."

His finger hovered above the control on his screen. "Are you sure?"

"You know pirates better than me," I said. "If you're sure, I'm sure."

Freddi had run with pirates for five years after the death of his wife. The way he was scared of them in that moment told me that the stories spacefarers tell about pirates are no exaggeration.

I braced myself for the explosion as Freddi touched the control.

Nothing.

"Drakh!"

Another clang.

Freddi looked up from the screen. There was fear in his eyes. "I'm sorry, Cassy. It's not working. I don't understand."

Ship's voice came over the speakers. "I'm getting an incoming transmission. It wants to take over my communication cir–"

All the screens in the control room flickered as her voice was abruptly cut off. The same image appeared on each of them: a large, impressive man with a confident grin and several large gold chains around his neck. "My name is Kadred." His voice filled the control room. "You may have heard of me."

I turned to Freddi. From the frightened look on his face, I knew he had heard the stories about Kadred as much as I had.

Kadred continued: "You also may have realised that I have secured limpet mines to your docking port – seeing as your ship decided not to invite me on board when I asked so nicely."

So Freddi was right about the clanging noises, not that it made me feel any better.

"Now," he said, as he twirled one of his gold chains like it was a casual, everyday conversation. "I could detonate the bombs and blast my way in, but that will create one vac of a mess and waste half a dozen bombs that I paid good money for. So I think it would be better for all concerned if you just let my fighters come on board and help themselves to what is going to be mine eventually anyway."

I glanced at Freddi and saw that his whole body was despondent. He nodded.

"Ship," I said. "Allow Kadred's people to dock."

"But Cassy, I don't think they're our friends," she said.

"I know, Ship. But let them dock anyway."

FREDDI GAVE ME a choice: either fight the pirates to the death or sit by and watch as they stripped everything of value from the ship that was our home.

I'm all for fighting to protect what's mine, but I wasn't foolish enough to take on a suicide mission.

We decided to wait in the control room. It was an obvious place for them to find us and to demonstrate that we offered no resistance. If we tried to run or hide, Freddi told me, we risked being hunted down and killed by an over-zealous pirate. Kadred had a reputation for not killing people unless he had to, but that didn't mean he wouldn't do it if pushed.

"I don't like this, Cassy," said Ship.

"I know, Ship," I said.

"They're heading straight for our qubition stores. If they take our qubition, how are we going to wormhole ever again?"

"It's okay, Ship," I said. "We'll buy more qubition, everything will be fine."

Not that I should be reassuring a ship that had no feelings. I looked at Freddi and twirled my finger near my head to suggest that Ship was going a little crazy.

He nodded and looked back at his screen. "There's also a group of them heading our way," he said. "As expected."

Within minutes there were three of them in the control room pointing their EE attack rifles in all directions to cover the space. They all wore clothes of the same style which, although civilian dress, made them almost a uniform. Their trousers and jackets were dark, mostly black, and of thick utilitarian material. Their hair was buzzed short to their heads and they each had a singular piece of gold jewellery. One of the men had a nose ring, the other had a ring through one ear. The third was a woman with a chunky gold necklace. Her body was so muscular, with the line of her breasts hidden under her jacket, that she seemed almost masculine. She pointed her gun at me with the supreme confidence of someone who was prepared to use it if provoked.

Freddi put his hands up to his shoulders with his empty palms facing outwards to show that he was unarmed. I followed his lead.

"Etchin!" said the woman and gestured with the point of her gun to indicate the man with the nose ring should go over to me.

I took an involuntary step backwards and felt my backside touch the physical barrier of the console behind. Then I saw the woman was looking at the weapon holstered to my leg and was instructing the man, whose name was evidently Etchin, to remove it.

The rank stench of Etchin's body odour contaminated my personal space as he reached around my waist and unbuckled the holster. He took a grab of my bum as he did it. I flinched and forced myself not to knee him in the groin.

He had a feel of my thigh as well, as he undid the strap.

"Just the gun, Etchin!" the woman barked at him.

His mouth widened into a sickly grin as he took my weapon away from me and stepped back to join his fellow pirates.

"You two," she ordered me and Freddi. "Over to the wall." She indicated the side of the control room with the tip of her gun. With our hands still raised, we stepped over the console panels on the floor to get to the side wall. I started to turn back round.

"Face the wall!"

I obeyed and looked at the metal. My heart was thumping like crazy. I so wanted to turn around and beat all three of them to a pulp. But I had no doubt I would be shot before I had taken more than one step.

I heard her approach us. She kicked my left leg apart from my right and began to search me. It was a professional search, she didn't touch me in any sexual way, she simply patted me down for weapons. I had none. Then she searched Freddi in the same, efficient manner. She found the knife he kept in the inside pocket of his waistcoat and stuffed it into the waistband of her trousers.

She took a step back and I heard her speak into what I assumed was some sort of communicator. "The control room is secure," she said. "Two crew. No resistance."

A male voice responded. It sounded like Kadred. "Message received."

We stood in silence for several long, horrible minutes. The muscles in my arms were aching so much it was beginning to be painful.

"Can I put my hands down now?" I asked.

"Fine," said the woman.

I lowered my hands slowly, in case one of the men hadn't heard her and tried to shoot me. The relief in my arms spread all the way up to the tense muscles in my neck. Out of the corner of my eye, I saw Freddi lower his hands too.

"Both of you," ordered the woman. "Sit down facing the wall with crossed legs like good little children. Stay quiet and still and this will all be over soon."

We did as we were told. I stole a glance across at Freddi. His face was impassive and I couldn't read his emotions.

The tension rose at the sound of approaching heavy footsteps.

I understood why when I heard Kadred's voice in the room. "Report!"

"No change," said the woman. "All is secure."

I heard movement behind me and it frustrated me that I couldn't see what was going on. Then I realised, to the left of me was one of the panels taken from a console with its buffed and shiny side facing up. It wasn't the most sophisticated mirror in the Rim, but if I turned my head a little bit towards it and looked out of the corner of my eye, it was enough reflection to see what was going on.

Kadred was at my console. He was looking at something on the screen which I couldn't see. He swore. He tapped at it with his fingers. He swore again. Then he turned abruptly and headed towards us. I turned my eyes front.

He grabbed Freddi's shoulder and spun him round on the floor so fast that he toppled over and had to put down a hand to steady himself. "Where have you hidden all your supplies?"

"We haven't hidden them anywhere," said Freddi.

"Don't be smart!" said Kadred. He swung his arm so the back of his hand struck Freddi in the face with such force it knocked him sideways. He pulled himself upright and clasped his jaw where he'd been hit.

"We left Serilla before we could pick up what we wanted," said Freddi. "There's only two of us, we don't need much in the way of supplies."

"Left or had to leave?" he said. He kicked at one of the console panels on the floor and sent it skimming across to the back wall where it clattered to a stop. "What happened in here?"

"Nothing happened in here," said Freddi.

Kadred swung the back of his hand across Freddi's face again. "Do you like being tortured for information? Because I can arrange it."

"Let's just say that you're not the first people to board the ship uninvited in recent days."

"Is that why you left Serilla without stocking up on supplies? Are you on the run from someone?" Kadred bent down and grabbed the collar of Freddi's shirt. He pulled him up from sitting and looked into his face. "Would you be worth a pretty little ransom?"

"Kadred!" said the woman suddenly.

"What?!" he growled.

"Another ship has just docked."

From the reflection in the panel, I could see she was standing by Freddi's console. She had to be reading the information off the screen.

"What?" said Kadred and threw Freddi back down on the floor. Freddi reached out his hands to soften the impact and landed in a crumpled heap.

"Are you okay?" I whispered.

"Yeah," he said as he clutched the red welt on the side of his face.

Kadred was standing next to the woman at the console. He towered over her, not only in stature, but also with the authority of his presence.

"The ship has the signature of the Fertillan Guard."

He pushed her aside and stepped forward to take charge of the console. "Don't be a vac-arse." He tapped at the screen. Then he hit it harder as if interrogating it with violence would yield a better answer.

"Kadred!" screamed a male voice over the pirate's communicator. "Fertillan Guards are–" A blast of what sounded like gunfire cut off his words. He didn't finish his sentence. Either he was too busy, or he was too dead.

"Vacking incompetent, drakh-for-brains, vac-arses!" Kadred kicked the console where the protective panel should have been and his foot went right inside the workings. Sparks flew up around his boot. He didn't seem to notice. Or care.

"Watch them!" he barked at the woman. Then he beckoned at the two men. "You two: with me!"

Kadred marched out of the control room with the two men flanking him: EE rifles at the ready.

I glanced across at Freddi and mouthed an unspoken question: *Fertillan Guard?*

He seemed as surprised as I was.

Looking around as best I could without attracting attention, I saw that in his haste to obey Kadred's orders, the man who had groped me had left my weapon – still holstered – on the floor by the exit. The possibility of grabbing it and shooting the only person guarding us was beginning to take shape in my mind. But Freddi saw me looking. He shook his head: not a good idea.

Indeed not. At least, not yet.

The woman tapped her hand on the screen of Freddi's console. She slapped it with her open palm. "Vac!" From her exasperation, I assumed that Kadred's frustrated boot had stopped it working. She moved onto my console. She only tapped it a couple of times before her worried expression intensified.

She was barely paying us any attention. I readied myself for the right moment to grab my gun.

The woman pulled at the left shoulder of her jacket and brought it close to her mouth. Her communicator had to be attached to the fabric in some way. "What's going on?"

"We're pulling out!" cried a female voice from her shoulder over the background of shouting and gunfire. "Fertillan Guard are everywhere. Kadred's in the ship's only escape vessel. The others are saying if we don't get out soon, he'll leave without us."

The woman let go of her jacket and grabbed her rifle tighter. She pointed it at us. Both of us had turned almost the whole way round to watch her, but she didn't seem to notice. She was probably worried that Kadred had abandoned her. If I were in her position, I'd be worried too.

"You can go, it's okay," Freddi told her. "We won't stop you."

She lifted her rifle at Freddi, her finger on the trigger ready to fire. His hands flew up in a defensive position.

"Maybe I should kill you first," she said.

"No!" said Freddi. He was trying to stay calm and not entirely succeeding. "Kadred wouldn't like that. He likes to leave people behind to enhance his reputation. Dead people can't spread stories about how it was pointless to fight back when Kadred attacked them."

She seemed to be weighing up what Freddi was saying as she lowered her rifle a little. But I think part of her knew that shooting us and running away was her safest course of action, especially if she lied to Kadred about allowing us to live.

The voice screamed again from her shoulder. "They're letting us leave! But we have to be on board within five minutes. This is a call to everyone: we're undocking in five minutes."

Panic flickered across the woman's face.

She raised the rifle again. I saw the fear in her eyes as she looked down the barrel at me. Fear of being left behind and fear of taking someone else's life. I returned her gaze with all the humanity within me; pleading for my life as I tried to convey – somehow – that I was a person whose life was worth saving.

A noise from outside the entrance to the control room startled her. She swung round with her rifle and paced steadily forward to investigate.

I took my chance and leapt sideways for my weapon. One hand encircled the grip, the other unclipped it from the holster and I pulled out the handgun as I had rehearsed it in my head.

The pirate woman fired at something outside: the blast boomed down the corridor and her body jolted at the recoil.

I knew my weapon was not as powerful as hers, and if I was going to fire, I would have to make it count. If I only wounded her – or worse, went for a smaller target like her head and missed – she could return fire and I'd be dead.

I glanced around at Freddi. He pulled himself up on his haunches and scampered to hide behind the nearest console.

I stepped lightly and slowly sideways to where the larger captain's console would provide better cover while also being closer to the target.

Gunfire echoed in the corridor. Not from her rifle, but from someone else's EE weapon with a still powerful, but higher pitched blast. She pressed her back against the side wall.

I ducked down behind the console, but kept my gaze on the woman and my gun raised.

She edged backwards, with her gun ready at her hip.

An unseen, chillingly familiar voice spoke from the corridor.

"You don't want to shoot me," he said. "I have a whole fleet of Fertillan Guard between here and any escape route you might try to take. You can take your chances with them, or you could lower your weapon and I can let you live."

The owner of the voice stepped into the control room and I saw what I already knew: it was Trevel.

He wore an armoured suit in the same brown as his regular uniform and a helmet with the blast shield down. His unmistakable intense eyes stared out from behind the protective barrier as he aimed his military-grade EE rifle at her head.

The woman backed away, but didn't let her gun drop even a millimetre. "How do I know if I can trust you?" she said.

An explosion shot from Trevel's rifle and the woman's body was thrown backwards as the blast ripped into her forehead. Bits of her brain sprayed out into the control room. Her body slammed hard on the floor followed by the rain of her own blood as the echo of the blast rang out around us. Trevel – his EEW still aimed at her – walked up to her corpse and prodded her lifeless stomach with the barrel to make sure she was dead.

"You can't trust me," he said.

I think I had made a sound when his gun went off. I had gasped – or maybe I screamed – I don't remember. Whatever noise it was, it was enough for him to know I was there.

"You can come out now," he declared to the room.

I stood up from behind the console with my hands above my head. I'm not ashamed to say I was shaking a little.

I was still holding my gun, but with an open palm and with my finger away from the trigger. I showed it to him as I made an exaggerated move of placing it on the floor and kicking it away.

"All of you can come out," said Trevel.

Freddi emerged from the console behind me: his hands raised.

"Well," said Trevel, looking at the two of us. "Isn't this unexpected."

Chapter Nine

PRINCE STEPHEN STROLLED into the control room as if it were his own palace. He was dressed in regular Fertillan Guard uniform, not the armour which Trevel wore. He had undoubtedly sat out the battle well away from any action.

Trevel had allowed me and Freddi to sit at the two far consoles while he worked from the captain's chair. As soon as I sat down at the place I was allocated, I felt something soft squash underneath me. I reached under my bottom and pulled out a bit of the pirate woman's brain that had landed on the chair. I felt sick. It didn't help that the smell of burnt flesh and the taste of iron from her blood still hung in the air.

Trevel stood to attention as Stephen approached him.

"How are we doing?" asked Stephen.

"Full sweep of the ship completed, Sire. No living pirate individuals on board. We have a couple of bodies which are being disposed of."

"Fertillan casualties?"

"A few wounded, Sire. That's all."

"Excellent," said Stephen.

"It is a good result, Commander. Kadred's people are determined fighters. We did well to catch them by surprise."

"What you're saying, Trevel, is that we were lucky to pick a fight with pirates that we could easily win. And you think that, as a general rule, we should leave dangerous pirate scum well alone."

"I do not think, Sire. I merely follow orders."

"Of course you do," said Stephen.

I let out a small cough to attract their attention. "Excuse me," I said, waving my hand at them like a nervous schoolgirl at the back of the classroom. "I don't want to sound ungrateful or anything, but what are you doing here?"

Stephen smiled in that superior way I had seen before. "We responded to your distress call."

"Distress call?" I said. "We didn't put out a distress call."

"Actually, we did," said Freddi. "I initiated it just before we were boarded. Sometimes pirates rip out your communications so you can't summon help before they've got clean away. It's usually repairable, but I didn't want to be stranded out in deep space with no fuel or supplies for too long. Although, I kind of expected to attract the attention of someone willing to sell us stuff at inflated prices once the pirates had gone, not a military force willing to fight them off."

"Lucky we came along, then," said Stephen.

"Yeah," I said, doubtfully. "Lucky."

"Well." He smiled. "Not actually lucky. I also made sure a

tracker was on your spaceship. Your distress call only allowed us to intervene sooner."

"I'm surprised you intervened at all," said Freddi.

I shot him a warning glance. I was surprised as well, but I wasn't going to look a gift horse in the mouth. At the end of the day, we were both alive and that was the way I preferred it.

"So," I said. "What happens now?"

Stephen, very kindly – or very deviously, depending on your point of view – agreed to tow us back to Fertillan space. Kadred had taken virtually all of our qubition and we had precious little ordinary fuel left. So we were forced to accept.

Freddi and I retreated to the crew lounge where he had sequestered some beer and we were able to spend a few moments alone.

Part of me knew that if I drank the beer it would make my already-thumping head worse eventually. But the other part of me craved its muscle-relaxing effect. My body was a jangle of nerves.

"I don't think they've found what they're looking for," said Freddi.

"What?" I said, lifting the beer to my lips. I tried to stop my hand from shaking as I did so, but my hand wouldn't obey.

"Whatever it was that Hoggard stole from them. That's why they put a tracker on us, that's why they came guns-blazing to our rescue. They didn't want Kadred getting his hands on it."

"Rubbish," I said. "They've searched the ship all over. Twice.

If Hoggard stole anything from them, he had it with him when he left and it was either taken from him by whoever killed him, or Trevel found it on his body."

"Then what's your explanation for the rescue? The Fertillan Guard protect the interests of Fertilla. They don't give a drakh about the likes of us, even if we are Fertillan citizens."

I didn't have an alternative explanation and I didn't have time to think of one before the door opened and Prince Stephen strolled in. "Is that beer?" he said, eyeing our glasses with interest.

"Yes," I said.

"Any more where they came from?" said Stephen.

"Uh, yeah," said Freddi. He slipped down off the couch and went to one of the store cupboards on the back wall.

The prince was making me feel uncomfortable the way he was standing next to me, rocking back and forth on his heels like he was impatient for something.

"Am I supposed to stand up or salute or something when you come into the room?" I asked him.

"If you were a member of the Fertillan Guard then, strictly, yes."

"Not curtsey or bow or something?"

"If I were carrying out my royal duties, as opposed to my military ones, there would be protocol, yes."

"It's just that," I babbled, "this is the first time we've actually met when you've not been arresting me or questioning me or having me searched."

He laughed. "I suppose."

Freddi returned with a beer and handed it to him. Stephen took it without seeming to care that Freddi had absolutely no intention of saluting or bowing before him.

Stephen took a long swig.

"Thank you," he said and wiped his lips on the sleeve of his uniform in a most un-royal-like fashion. "We've secured the tether to your ship and should be ready to leave soon. Are you sure you want to be taken to this Fancy woman?"

I sniggered.

"Nanci," corrected Freddi.

"Yes please," I said.

"There are more qualified people to repair your ship on Fertilla," said Stephen. "I'm sure I can get a recommendation for you."

"No thank you," said Freddi abruptly. He clearly didn't like royalty and had no intention of hiding it. "Nanci knows us, and she owes us. We prefer to go there."

"If that's what you prefer," conceded Stephen.

The conversation stopped. I gripped my glass tighter, feeling the beer getting warm under my increasingly sweaty palm.

"Well," said Freddi after a moment. "I should make sure the tether is secure this end and oversee the towing procedure."

Stephen waved a dismissive hand. "My people will do that."

"I'm sure they will," said Freddi. "But I've looked after this ship for many years, I'd like to make sure."

"If you wish," said Stephen. He said it like he was giving permission.

I watched Freddi leave. I'd hoped he would look behind so I could throw a pleading glance not to be left alone with the prince. Maybe he could make up some ruse and call me away to help him with something he didn't really need any help with. But he didn't turn back and once the door had closed, there was just the two of us.

Stephen stepped sideways and rested one hand on the back of

the couch in the relaxed way someone might in their own home. Whether it was conscious or not, it gave the impression that he regarded himself in charge, even though it was my ship. Meanwhile, I stood before him with all the nerves of a courtier on her first day.

"So," said Stephen. "How does the daughter of a seamstress and a technician come to be captain of her own ship?"

I felt uncomfortable standing in front of him, like I was still under interrogation. "You looked me up?"

"Standard procedure," he said.

"I inherited the ship," I said.

He turned his head sideways as he watched me and waited for me to reveal more. "From whom? All your family were Fertillan-based, none of them were spacefarers."

He really had looked me up. "I knew the previous captain," I explained. "When he died, he left the ship to me."

"Very generous of him."

"We…" I remembered Alix's face and it awakened the pain of knowing I will never see it for real again. "We had a relationship."

Alix was my friend, my confidante, my lover. We met when he stopped off on Fertilla after a freight run and we instantly found a connection. We shared dreams of travelling the Rim together in his ship; taking whatever jobs were on offer to visit whatever planets or systems we desired. Friends said I was naive. They said I was carried away with the romance of it all. But I loved him, I really did, and I still miss him.

"How did he die?" said Stephen.

It was a blunt and unfeeling question, but then a man in his position was used to not having to take people's feelings into account.

"He took on a job he shouldn't have," I said. "Vacked off the wrong person and got killed for it."

I was there when he was shot on the smuggler's vessel. I saw the terror in his face when he realised the blast was heading for his chest and I saw the light fade from his eyes after it obliterated his heart. His body was dumped out of an airlock and sent into the nearest sun. I was lucky the smugglers let me live. But I was a pathetic creature back then – sobbing so hysterically I could barely stand – and I don't think they saw me as a threat. I toughened up pretty quickly after that.

"That's why I make sure all my jobs are legit," I said. "The illegal stuff pays well, but the risks are too great."

"And Frederus Aaron? You two seem close."

"Freddi?" I couldn't help but smile at the thought of me and Freddi together. "Freddi's just… Well, he's *Freddi*. He came with the ship. That is, Alix had employed him and he was working on the ship when I inherited it. I was going to drop him off somewhere and he was going to get another job, but somehow we never got round to it."

The ship jolted and I lost my balance; stumbling right into Stephen's personal space. He grabbed my arm to steady me and, as I restored my footing, he gently let go.

"I think we're underway," he said. "Perhaps sitting down would be best."

Stephen sat on the couch and leant sideways with one arm draped across the back cushion.

The ship jolted again. I didn't stumble this time, but spilled some of my beer which ran in a cold trickle down my arm.

"I can highly recommend sitting," said Stephen.

He was right. I sat next to him and drank the rest of my beer to calm my nerves.

He drank his beer too.

"Aren't you going back to your ship?" I asked.

"I'm on the communicator if they need me," he said. "Which they won't. It's a standard flight back to Fertilla."

"I see," I said. I really didn't. Things can go wrong even on a standard flight and the senior ranking officer should be there to take charge when they do. Not drinking beer on a civilian ship being towed behind them.

"I wanted to ask you about my father," he said.

"I told you," I said. "I didn't know your father."

"Then how do you explain him putting your name on a protected list?"

"I don't. A lot of things went haywire after the plague, if the records are that old, then…"

"Maybe," he said. He finished his beer and looked at the bottom of the glass as if not quite believing it was empty. "Do you have any more?"

"I don't know. Freddi's the custodian of the beer. But I know where he keeps it, I'll have a look."

I took both his glass and mine over to the cupboard and took the last of Freddi's stash.

Returning, I again sat next to the prince on the couch.

Was I already getting a little drunk? On just one beer? Maybe all the adrenaline my body pumped into my system during the pirate attack was exaggerating the effect of the alcohol.

Stephen drank like a thirsty man. "In a way, it was the plague that killed my father."

"It was?" That wasn't the way I remembered lessons about the Regellan royal family at school. "I thought he survived the plague."

He smiled. "I forget sometimes that parts of my life are public domain. Yes, you're right. He survived the plague, but he had been very ill and it weakened his lungs. So when he caught pneumonia, he succumbed quickly. I was very young."

"Do you remember him at all?" I said.

"I have one memory from when he became sick. His skin was pale and he coughed like his lungs wanted to escape his chest. I was whisked away from him when the staff realised what was going on and promised that I could see him again when he got better. He never got better, of course."

"No," I said.

I saw past his uniform again and into the man who sat next to me. Perhaps it was a side of himself he could not show on his own ship where he was Marshal Commander Stephen Regellan. Perhaps that was why he was sitting on my couch and drinking Freddi's beer.

"What about you, Sesaan?"

I flinched at the use of my first name. "People usually call me Cassy."

"I'm sorry, Cassy," he said. "I'm Stephen."

"I don't think I can call you Stephen, Sire."

"It's easy," he said. "It's only two syllables."

I laughed. I'm not entirely sure why I laughed. Perhaps it was the beer.

We talked some more and laughed some more. I almost forgot I was talking to a prince. It was such a release after everything that had happened.

I can't even remember what we were laughing about when Freddi came back.

"Cassy, I wonder if you can come down to the engine room, I want you to have a look at…" He trailed off as he saw us both relaxed sitting next to each other on the couch.

Like he had interrupted something.

Maybe he had.

Instinctively, I sat up a little straighter.

Stephen stood. "I should check in with my people anyway." He tugged his jacket smooth as if restoring his authority. "If you'll excuse me."

Stephen marched off and the military man in him reasserted itself steadily with each stride.

We waited until he had gone. "What's up with the engines?" I asked.

"Nothing," said Freddi. "I thought you might need rescuing, that's all."

"Thank you, but I was actually fine."

"So I saw."

"What?"

"You and the prince… together on the sofa." He gave me a knowing wink.

"Oh, don't talk rubbish!"

"I'm only saying."

"Come on, let's head down to the engine room. I need to see how much damage the pirates did. We can do that from down there."

Chapter Ten

Prince Stephen's ship dropped us off within the security fire-wall that surrounds Fertilla to allow us to transmit a message to Nanci to warn her we were coming. Her station sits in a wide orbit around the planet and is a sprawling mass of modules and nondescript add-ons that give it an irregular and random-looking outline. If you asked Nanci, she would say that every addition is a vital part of her establishment. If you asked most other people, they would say she collects bits and pieces she doesn't know what to do with and finds a use for them later.

Nanci welcomed Freddi with a greasy handshake and me with a hug that squeezed me tight against her ample breasts. She said she would suspend her other work while she supervised a team to assess the damage on our ship. She offered us both tea and suggested we wait in her office. The tea wasn't the expensive real stuff, but a brown watery substance spat out from a machine. At least it helped with dehydration.

I drank the wet and warm liquid and held the cup in my hands until it went cold. Freddi and I soon ran out of things to talk about and I ended up looking around at the chaotic belongings Nanci had stuffed into her office. Very like looking at the outside of her station, it was a magpie's nest of bits and pieces. Most of them were from spaceships and looked vaguely familiar, while some of them almost certainly weren't. I was most intrigued by what looked like an oval-shaped pump on her desk with tubes sticking out of it that I could have sworn was some sort of artificial heart. She was using it as a paperweight for a pile of documents stacked haphazardly on one side. An unusually large pile for an office with five screens mounted in the desk and on the walls. More than enough computers for her to carry out her work without the need for an expensive commodity like paper.

By the time Nanci came shuffling back into her office, my bum had gone numb from sitting for so long and I was starting to need a pee from drinking her surprisingly potent tea.

Freddi and I stood up: anxious for news.

She looked up from the P-tab she was carrying. "I found out why your ship says she loves you," said Nanci.

Freddi opened his mouth to say something, but Nanci continued before he had a chance.

"And it's not because you are especially loveable, Frederus. She had a little bit of malware bouncing around her operating system."

"Malware?" I said, not really understanding.

"Yes, very odd," said Nanci and stopped like that was all the explanation required.

"Like a virus?" I asked.

"Sort of."

"How did it get there?"

"Someone put it there, I should imagine," said Nanci.

I glanced at Freddi, who didn't look like he was getting it either. "I think what Cassy means," he said, "is why would anyone do that?"

"Ordinarily, I would say because they think it's funny or a game or a challenge. But in this case, I think they put it there so you would find it," said Nanci. "Have you had any suspicious characters on board your ship recently?"

I nodded, regretfully. "Just a few."

"Well, there you go then," she said, again as if no further explanation was required.

"Can you repair it?" asked Freddi.

"Repair it?" said Nanci. "It's repaired. Once I found the culprit, I extracted it without an issue. As I say, when I knew what I was looking for, it was easy to find. It appears to be some kind of coded document with a little program which wormed its way into Ship's behavioural circuits causing her to come over all romantic. It was crudely done. Whoever did it was either in a hurry or not very expert. Possibly both."

A shiver went through me when Nanci mentioned a code. Hoggard's dying words were: 'deliver the code'. It couldn't be a coincidence.

He had to be the one who had hidden it on the ship.

He had to be the one who messed with Ship's behavioural program.

"What does the document say?" I asked Nanci.

"Ah," she said. "That's where who-ever-it-was was a bit more clever. It's encrypted. I ran it through a few de-coding programs out of my own curiosity, but came up with nothing.

You'll need a specialist to crack it."

She delved into her pocket and pulled out a memory ball which she placed on her desk. The silver sphere rolled slowly away from her until it hit a coil of wire and came to rest. "I saved it for you. If someone went to all that trouble to first encrypt it, then ensure you found it, I'm thinking it's probably important."

I picked up the sphere – it was warm from being in Nanci's pocket – and clasped it in my palm.

Now that I had the code Hoggard talked about, it scared me.

I secreted the memory ball into my pocket where it would have to stay until I decided what the vac to do about it.

CHAPTER ELEVEN

With Kadred having stolen our ship's only shuttle, Nanci agreed to lend us a short hop vessel to get down to Fertilla. She would, "put it on the bill," she said.

The repairs we needed were not complicated, but sourcing a new (well, second hand) shuttle to replace the one we lost was likely to take time. She also said she would refuel the ship and stock us up on qubition. None of this was cheap and I agreed to reduce the scale of the cosmetic work I had originally wanted done. But not in my room. I couldn't go in there every day and be reminded of the way it had been searched by the Fertillan Guard.

All of which meant we had time to kill on Fertilla.

Freddi said he would take the opportunity to visit his daughters on their farm. He invited me, but I said I might join him later. I had stuff to do in Londos. Not least, decide what to do about the memory ball in my pocket.

I MADE ARRANGEMENTS to stay with Mandi. We didn't have the best relationship, but she was the nearest thing I had to a family and her house, on the fringes of Londos's over-populated centre, was convenient.

Mandi greeted me with a mater-of-fact, "Ah, Cassy, you're here," and let me inside.

My first thought was how old Mandi had become. She was still as thin as a lamppost, but was becoming gaunt with her skin starting to sink between her bones and muscles. Unlike the inside of her house, which had been given a fresh look with recently painted walls and polished floors. It was hard to believe there were once up to ten children living there at any one time – most of them orphans from the plague going through some sort of bereavement.

Mandi didn't foster children much any more, she told me as she took me up to my room. She preferred adults. They don't stay as long and they paid her more for the privilege. I took the hint that I was expected to settle my bill in full, despite our previous relationship.

It was odd stepping into my old room. Where there used to be four small beds crammed into the space, there was now one adult-sized double pressed up against the window. Where a rickety old wardrobe had once leant into the corner, there stood a new wardrobe with a door that didn't look like it was going to fall off. Where some of the children had left greasy fingermarks on the walls, there was now clean, white paint. It was so much more welcoming than when I had first walked in and realised, with horror, that I would be sharing it with three other girls. I was so young then, maybe three or four. Not that I can ever be sure as my birthday wasn't recorded in the chaos after the plague.

I knelt up on the bed and looked out of the window like I had done as a child. It was the same old view of the street with people rushing by and the row of houses opposite. I wondered if it was such a great idea coming back, even if it was convenient.

Then Mandi called me for dinner and I went downstairs.

THE DINING ROOM felt too big to have just me in it and the table was definitely too large. There were six place settings and only the two of us, as I gathered Mandi kept the table set in case she had last-minute guests.

"How is space?" Mandi shouted through from the kitchen as she clattered about, putting together our meal.

"Space is fine," I called back.

"Haven't got yourself killed then, yet?"

"Not yet."

Mandi came through with two plates of cold food. Each of us had a hunk of bread, a long chunky carrot with the green bits still on the top (although mine had started to go a bit brown), a soggy-looking onion and a ball of something soft and yellow.

She sat down opposite me and gave me a big, self-satisfied smile. "I managed to get some butter," she said.

That's what the soft and yellow ball was. I eagerly spread it on my bread. I considered putting a thin layer across the whole of it, but instead decided to do a big dollop on one corner so I could really taste it.

I took a bite and the heat of my mouth melted the butter; releasing its slick saltiness across my tongue. It was heavenly. I chewed slowly, eking out every bit of flavour until there was no more to have, before swallowing and allowing my stomach to make a start on extracting its nutrients.

Once I had eaten the bread, I was left with the carrot and what turned out to be a pickled onion. I wish I had eaten my meal the other way round so I had finished with wonderful tastes still lingering in my mouth. But I had been too keen and had to allow the dull taste of the carrot to dilute the creaminess of the butter and then the pickled onion to obliterate it altogether.

"How long are you planning to stay?" said Mandi.

"A few days," I said. "Maybe a week. Depends how long the repairs take on my ship."

Mandi nodded. Unlike me, she had saved her bread till last and was smearing a knife full of butter across its surface in a thin layer.

"While I'm here waiting, I thought I might look up some of the old crowd," I said.

"Mmm?" said Mandi, taking a mouthful of bread.

"Do you remember a boy called Nick?"

She swallowed and tapped her knife on the side of the plate as if it might help jog her memory. "Nick," she said. "No, don't think I remember a Nick."

"Bit of a whizz-kid with programming, grew up to work with Londos Corp on the environment control systems."

"Ah *Nick!*" said Mandi. "The sultry boy who grew his hair long to hide his sticky-out ear."

I laughed at the description. Yeah, that was him. "Do you know where he is now?"

"Hmm." She thought and tapped her knife again. "Some of the kids send me thank you messages once a year – the foster agency encourages it, apparently. They say it gives people a sense of family. I say it's a way of pulling on the heart strings of old fools like me to persuade them to keep taking in the little urchins. So I don't read them. You can have a look through if you like, maybe he sent one with a way to contact him."

"That would be great."

"Now where did I put my…?" She went out of the room muttering to herself and came back with a P-tab.

She transferred a file to my P-tab and took our plates into the kitchen where she clattered about clearing up.

The file, titled *Kids' Thank yous*, was full of messages from ex-foster children going back years, sorted in date and name order. For someone who claimed she didn't read them, she had made a not inconsiderable effort to keep them safe.

I resisted the temptation to walk down memory lane – and read messages meant for someone else – and scrolled through until I found a message from Nickolat Allette. It was a few years old, but at the bottom of a list of standard platitudes (hope you are well, the new job's going fine etc) was a business address for him in Londos.

Perfect.

The artificial lights of Londos had been dimmed to simulate the approaching night by the time I reached the run-down business district where Nick was based, according to the message. Londos, like most enclosed towns or centres of human population, opted to follow a twenty-four-hour day to mimic the rotation of SolPrime where the human race had evolved. Only farmers paid much attention to the much longer Fertillan day and even they kept roughly to a twenty-four-hour sleep/wake pattern.

The door to Nick's workshop, squeezed inconspicuously between two other buildings, was ajar. I knocked and stepped inside. "Hello?"

There was no answer, just the faint sound of music coming from above.

I was in an entranceway that offered me only two options: go back outside or walk up the set of stairs ahead of me. I chose to go up.

The music got louder with each step and revealed itself to be a modern popular tune I didn't recognise, with a wailing female vocal.

Reaching the top, I entered a room not much larger than my old childhood bedroom at Mandi's place, except it had no window and was far messier. In the centre was a workbench heaving with computer equipment which appeared to be the source of the music. A man's slightly out of tune voice was singing along, although the man himself wasn't visible.

"Hello? Nick?"

The singing stopped. A man stood up from behind the workbench. I recognised him immediately. He was older and taller than the boy I remembered, but it was definitely Nick. He still had long brown hair, but he had pulled it back into a ponytail, allowing his sticky-out ear to stick out as much as it liked.

"Music off!" he said, and the sound of the wailing female vocalist abruptly ceased. "Yes?"

"Hi, I wonder if you remember me. I'm Cassy. Sesaan Cassandra."

He seemed puzzled. He was looking straight at me, but there was not a hint of recognition in his face.

"From Mandi's house," I said.

That hit a memory. "Mandi?"

"She was the one who gave me your address, actually."

"I didn't think I was that hard to find. My business is fully advertised."

"I didn't know how to look you up," I said. "I tried searching for a boy with long hair called Nick, but I didn't get very far."

I smiled at my half-joke, but he wasn't smiling. "It's nice you found me, but you can tell Mandi I'm not loaning her any more money. It's time I should be closing up anyway, so I'll show you out."

He reached down under his bench and pulled out a brown canvas bag which he stuffed a few things into.

"Mandi didn't send me," I said.

He seemed not to care as he slung his bag over his shoulder and began picking his way across the room to the doorway.

"There's something I need help with." I reached into my pocket and pulled out the memory ball. "I remember you had a gift for programming and I thought you might be able to decrypt something for me."

He was standing in front of me now. He was quite a bit taller than me and much more muscular than his under-nourished childhood body suggested he would ever become. As he looked at me close up, his expression slowly changed into one of recognition.

"I remember you now," he said. "You didn't lose everyone in the plague like the rest of us. Your mother was killed in a fire. You were small and timid and everyone said we had to be nice to you because you'd recently lost your mum in a horrific way. And I remember thinking, well I watched my mum cough her lungs out for days while the plague gradually sapped the life from her body and no one was ever nice to me. They just bolted our door shut so we couldn't come out and spread the disease to other people."

"I'm sorry." I felt embarrassed; guilty.

"Not your fault. It was a bad time." He looked down at the memory ball in my hand, its silver coating shiny under the lights of his workshop. "What have you got there?"

"It's a memory ball."

"I can see it's a memory ball."

"I found some code on my ship, but it's encrypted and I don't know what it is."

"Well, I'm off home. It's the kids' club night and it's the only time I can get some peace. I'd say I'd have a look for you tomorrow, but with the amount of work I've got on at the moment…"

He squeezed past me and headed off down the stairs.

I had to run down the steps to keep up with him. "Then, can you recommend someone? I have a few contacts myself, but they're not on Fertilla and I'm kind of stuck here until my ship can be repaired."

I followed Nick out of the door and into the street. "There are few places," he said. "You're best calling round some of them, to be honest."

He pulled the door shut and pressed his hand on the lockpad. I heard bolts shoot out into the doorframe.

"It's just that I'd like to keep the whole thing quiet," I said. "You know, off the books."

I feared I had said too much. I had no reason to trust him any more than anyone else.

He raised his eyebrows at me. "Off the books?"

"It could be nothing," I said, trying to backtrack a little. "But knowing the man who left it, I want to be careful."

Nick opened his palm. It took me a moment to realise he was asking for the memory ball. I dropped the silver sphere into his hand.

He turned it in his fingers while he thought for a moment. "Maybe I can take a look."

"You'll do it?" I said.

"Encryption isn't programming. If it's a really tough nut to crack, you're going to need an encryption expert. But yeah, I'll do it. Give me several days and I'll send you a message when I'm done."

Chapter Twelve

I RETURNED TO MANDI's house feeling both excited and nervous. Excited at the prospect of finding out what was in Hoggard's code and nervous about what I was going to do about it when I did.

Both emotions doubled when I checked my messages before bed.

One was from the Regellan royal household and looked very official indeed:

His Royal Highness, Prince Stephen Regellan of Fertilla, requests the company of Individual Sesaan Cassandra at Londos House tomorrow at 3pm for afternoon tea, it said. *Confirmation is not required as attendance is assumed.*

Courtier D. Brimble

LITTLE GIRLS ARE supposed to dream about receiving an invitation from a prince, but my childhood fantasies never stretched to something so grand. When I wasn't dreaming that my mum and dad were still alive and would come and get me so we could live together as a family, I was dreaming of flying off into space and having adventures.

So I never thought about what I would do should I ever be summoned to the palace. I never thought about wearing a beautiful dress and a tiara and tottering about on impossible shoes to make myself seem attractive to His Royal Highness.

Just as well, because I would have been disappointed. I only owned one dress and that was old, faded and back on the ship. On Fertilla, I had the shirt and trousers I was wearing the day before or a clean shirt and pair of trousers.

I opted for the clean ones.

Finding my way to Londos House was easy as it is a very well known building in the centre of the town. It is not only the home of King Richard, but also to his brothers Prince James and, of course, Prince Stephen. In the years before the governing family of Fertilla decided to bestow royalty on themselves, it was the administrative hub for the planet. But, over time, most of the administration staff were moved out to other buildings and the royal family took it over to be their grand home.

To describe it as a 'palace' in the old sense of the word would be misleading. It is merely a large house, very similar to most other houses on Fertilla, apart from its size and the fact that it is kept in impeccably good order. It is also guarded by a squadron of very visible Fertillan Guards who patrol the grounds with the determination of troops who have a marching exam coming up that they need to practise for.

One glared at me from beneath the peak of her cap when I approached. But she conceded that I was expected and took me to a thin weaselly man known as Courtier Brimble. He was dressed in such an anachronistic costume that I might have thought he was a projection from a history play if it wasn't for the sound of his wheezy breathing. His jacket and trousers were black and completely unwrinkled other than for a single, crisp crease down the front of each trouser leg and along the top of each sleeve. His shirt was bright white and also unwrinkled and was secured at the neck with an item of clothing I believed was called a 'tie'. The knot, which was tied tight at the throat, appeared to be designed to keep the collars of his shirt close to his neck to keep it warm in the absence of buttons. Except that Londos House was far from cold and the buttons on the rest of his shirt seemed to be functioning perfectly.

"Have you met the prince before?" he asked.

"I sort of have," I said.

"Either you have or you haven't," he wheezed. "It's a simple question: have you or have you not met the prince before?"

"I have. Just not formally."

"I presume you know how to greet him. Show me your curtsey."

"My what?"

This was the royal protocol which Stephen had referred to on the ship and about which I was totally clueless. It was all a pack of nonsense as far as I was concerned, but to Courtier Brimble it was supremely important and he wouldn't take me a step further inside until he was satisfied I could curtsey with appropriate reverence.

At last, he took me through to the inner sanctum of the Regellan household.

It was truly breathtaking.

The space was the first thing I noticed, as the rather plain and perfunctory corridor opened up into a room the size of my ship's cargo hold. Only much more ostentatious. Everything inside had a vibrant colour, and yet none of it clashed. At the centre was a table the size of Mandi's dining table, but at calf height and made in a shiny golden brown material that might even have been real wood. Three sofas of a golden yellow with plush embroidered cushions surrounded it and on every surface there were ornaments and pictures that few ordinary people would even dream of owning.

I was so busy gawping at all the stuff in the room that I almost missed Prince Stephen walking towards me. He looked totally relaxed out of his uniform, in loose black trousers and billowing white shirt with a waistcoat of shiny black material embroidered with gold thread.

I curtsied as I had been taught, even though I felt foolish.

Stephen was unfazed. "Thank you, Brimble," he said.

"Sire," said Brimble. He bowed and backed out.

I heard the door click shut behind me and raised myself back to standing.

"Glad you could come, Cassy," he said.

"By the sound of the invitation, I didn't think I had a choice," I said.

"You always have a choice. Unless I am arresting you." He chuckled at his own joke.

"You're not, though? Going to arrest me?"

"I thought I would offer you some tea. Do you like tea?"

"Um, yes."

Stephen got Brimble to return with a tray containing a surfeit of fine crockery. There was a cup for each of us which had its own little plate to sit on (a 'saucer', apparently), we each had a small spoon for use with the tea (a 'teaspoon') which, to prevent drips on the tray, rested on its own mini-plate (a 'teaspoon rest'), there was a small pot of honey should we require sweetness, while the tea itself was contained in an ample teapot with the steam from its hot contents drifting out in a plume which swirled into the air.

Brimble placed the tray on the table. "Would you like me to pour, Sire?"

"No no," said Stephen, waving the servant away. "I'm perfectly capable of lifting a teapot."

Brimble left and Stephen offered me a seat on the large yellow sofa beside the table. As I sat, I felt its plump cushions soften around me. Stephen sat next to me and the sofa didn't so much as tip in his direction as he added his weight.

"You really did invite me here to drink tea," I said.

"It's a royal tradition." He picked up the pot and poured two steaming cups of golden brown liquid. Even the tea, I noted, fitted in with the colour scheme of the room. "Help yourself to honey."

I don't usually have anything in my tea, but honey is rare and expensive, so I helped myself to a spoonful and watched it melt into the hot liquid in my cup as I stirred.

"I actually invited you for a chat," said Stephen. "But that doesn't fit royal protocol."

"And tea does?"

"Quite so."

I lifted the cup to my lips, but it was too hot to drink, so I lowered it again. Stephen's tea, I noticed, was still on the tray and he hadn't added any honey.

"I enjoyed our chat on your ship," he explained.

"Are you sure it wasn't Freddi's beer you enjoyed?"

"That too." He smiled. "I don't get to socialise with many ordinary people in my life. They're mostly courtiers like Brimble, or guardsmen. Either way, it's always 'yes, Sire' this and 'yes, Sire', that. It's very refreshing to talk to someone like you."

I wasn't sure whether to be flattered or insulted, and in the confusion ended up feeling embarrassed. I covered my emotion with a sip of tea. This time, it was cool enough and I got an unexpected hit of sweet honey.

"Don't you meet ordinary people when you're with the Fertillan Guard?"

"Rarely. That little adventure chasing Andrus Hoggard off-planet was unusual. My role, as head of the Fertillan Guard, is overseeing planetary security, especially royal security, and involves far too much administration. I put myself on active duty as often as I can, but my squadron is very protective of me. I think they fear if anything happens to me, being a royal prince and everything, it's going to be their neck. They're probably right, to be fair."

He picked up his cup of tea and drank it down in one large swig. Then he picked up the teapot and poured himself another.

He continued: "At the moment I'm supposed to be overseeing the security for Andrus Hoggard's funeral. Can you believe it? A traitor who stole secrets from us and they want a royal presence at his funeral? Apparently, as he was working for the royal household, it's protocol. To not attend would be to admit that we had a security breach and that would be an embarrassment."

"Is that why you were chasing him? Because he stole 'secrets'?"

I had hoped to get more information out of him about the code hidden on my ship, but Stephen continued to be vague. "That's what James told me. The Deity knows what they were because James was livid. He blames me, of course. The whole point of putting me in charge of royal security, he says, was to stop this sort of thing happening. He's only trying to pass the blame because Hoggard was working for him and he screwed up. He needs to keep a tighter rein on his staff, I told him. But no, it's still apparently my fault. So James and I are going to Hoggard's funeral under the pretence that the man died in a street mugging that went wrong while on a diplomatic mission to Serilla."

"He's dead. Does it matter?" I said.

"It gives some comfort to his widow, I suppose." He drank down his second cup of tea – again, all in one. "Not as if you came here to listen to me moaning about my family."

"I don't mind," I said. I liked listening to him, even when he was moaning. It was a weird feeling.

"I actually have something to show you." He got up off the sofa and looked around the room. "Now where the vac is it? That's the trouble with having staff who clean up after you, they move things and you can never find them – aha!"

Stephen picked up a P-tab which was on a mantlepiece at the back of the room. He put it on the table as he sat back down on the sofa. I looked at its blank screen and wondered what he was going to show me.

"I did some looking into the protected list my father put you on," he said. "I checked the dates: you're right, you were just a child when he died. It didn't make sense. I thought about what you said about everything going haywire after the plague, and it's true that record keeping wasn't the highest priority at that time. Even so, I had another look at your file and I'm as sure as I can be that it was my father who put the note there and that he meant to do it. Then I remembered something–"

He picked up the P-tab and its screen came to life. His fingers played on its surface. But he was sitting up the other end of the sofa to me and he had brought the screen up to his face so all I could see was its plain, unedifying back cover.

"–something that made your face seem familiar," he said.

His eyes lifted from the P-tab and he looked right at me. Like he was studying my face.

I felt embarrassed again, but also a little excited at his gaze.

He returned his attention to the screen. "That's the other reason I wanted to see you again in person. To compare you to this."

He put the P-tab down on the table to reveal an old photograph. It was very obviously a picture of King John standing in the very same room in which we were sitting. At his feet sat a large woolly animal I believed to be a dog and by his side stood a plainly dressed woman.

"Do you think she looks like you?"

The photograph drew me in as I stared at the woman with the same long dark hair as me, the same thin lithe body shape as me and the same brown eyes that I see in the mirror. "That's my mother," I said under my breath.

"I thought it might be," said Stephen.

"But…?" I looked at him. I looked back at the photograph. Thoughts whirled through my mind; none of them making sense. "Where did you get this?"

"It's part of the family collection. I used to look at them as a boy so I wouldn't forget what my father looked like."

"But this can't be my mother. My mother didn't have anything to do with royalty."

"Maybe she did," said Stephen. "I checked the old staff lists for her name and couldn't find it, but like you say, record keeping went a little haywire after the plague."

"That doesn't explain why your father put me on a protected list."

"My father was notoriously generous to the staff," said Stephen. "My mother was born to be queen, whereas my father married into royalty. I don't think he made the transition easily."

"I don't understand."

"Your father was a plague victim, right?"

"Yeah."

"I'm sorry. It must have been tough for you."

He really did look sorry. In that moment, I felt a connection to him and not just because both of us had lost our fathers. It was something more than that, something that made me want to get close to him. Something I hadn't felt since those far off days when I first met Alix.

I tried to shake it off and not think about it. "I don't remember him," I said. "He died before I was born."

"I can see why my father might have felt sorry for your mother, bringing you up on her own. I wouldn't put it past him to say he'd look out for you. Putting that note on your file would have been easy for him. He was King, after all."

I looked again at the picture of my mother standing with the King. He was staring directly at the camera without regard for either my mother or the dog beside him. He was proud, regal, even superior.

She looked sad. It's how I remember her. A woman burdened by the loss of her husband and struggling to bring up a child on her own. I looked deeper into her eyes and tried to understand more. But it was only a picture; a snapshot in time. It merely told me she had once stood with the King in the same room as I now sat with the prince. I couldn't ask it to tell me any more than that, just as I could not ask the people in it – the King, my mother, and presumably the dog, were all dead.

Chapter Thirteen

THE IMAGE OF my mum's face from the old photograph played in my mind after I returned to Mandi's and I couldn't sleep. Eventually, I sat up in bed and pulled out the few old pictures I had of her and spent the last hours of the night looking at them. They were so familiar I could have retrieved them from my memory rather than my P-tab, but I tried to look at them afresh. I hadn't realised that, as I had got older, my face was growing to look more like hers. I hoped it resembled the best picture I had of her, with Dad on their wedding day when there was still light in her eyes, rather than the later ones where I saw the loneliness inside of her.

I got up as the lights of Londos got brighter and signalled morning. With the day, came the opportunity to find out more about my mother's past than I had been told as a child. I asked Mandi, but she said she knew nothing more than I did: my mother was a widow, she worked as a seamstress and she died in a fire. If the fostering agency had told her any more, she had forgotten it.

With the rest of my family either dead or so distant they hadn't even known my mother, I realised that the only lead was the clothing factory where she was employed. If it still existed, and if I could find it, there was a chance that one of her former colleagues might remember her.

Fertillan records, such that they were, suggested that the factory was still in business and gave me an address to try. It took me twice as long to get there than it should have done because the streets of Londos had changed over the years and I took several wrong turns.

But eventually, I arrived at an industrial area with larger premises than the business district where I had found Nick's workshop. It was busy at that time of day with lots of people arriving for work. I was about to check the address again on my P-tab when I realised, looking around, that all the units had signs above them proclaiming what they were. '*Bespoke Clothing – Quality at a Price You Can Afford*' was one such sign which, although faded, clearly related to a doorway where a stream of people, mostly women, were arriving in ones and twos.

They were almost all young women at that, not old enough to remember my mother, and a lot of them younger than me.

I stopped one of them. "Excuse me," I said. "I was wondering–"

"I'll get the manager," said the woman without waiting for me to finish, and rushed inside.

The manager turned out to be an older woman. Much older, with long hair which had turned naturally grey and was swept up into a ponytail on top of her head. It was difficult to tell if she could be the right age to have known my mother or not. The photographs I had, preserved the image of my mother as a young woman who never had the opportunity to grow old.

"Yes?" said the manager with the abruptness of someone who had been interrupted doing something important. "Are you chasing an order or making an order?"

"It's not actually about an order," I said.

"Did you want our catalogue? I can send you our catalogue." She reached into the pocket of her long pencil skirt and pulled out a P-tab.

"I actually had a question about my mother." I pulled up a picture of her on my own P-tab and showed it to the manager. "She used to work here, do you remember her?"

"Oh," said the woman. The disappointment in her voice was plain as she lowered her P-tab and stuck it back in her pocket. "You're Isabette's child."

"Yes!" I was so excited I almost dropped my P-tab. "Isabette Cassandra. Do you remember her?"

"I remember she died in that awful fire," said the manager. "I thought her kid burnt to death too. Glad to hear the stories were wrong."

"What was she like? What did she do here? Did she have friends? Do some of them still work here?" The questions fired from my mouth like repeated blasts from an EE gun. I had gone there to ask about the photograph Stephen had shown me. I hadn't thought about what it would be like to meet someone who had actually known my mother. An adult who might have talked to her, laughed with her, understood her better than I could ever have done as a young child.

"She was a pain in the arse," said the manager. "We lost a lot of good work because of her. I should have sacked her."

Her words tore the heart out of me. I remembered my mother as kind and loving, sad and lonely. She had given me the only bit of inner goodness I had to hold onto while I grew up with the feral kids at Mandi's place. This woman's description was so alien to my memory that it had to be untrue.

"My mother was Isabette Cassandra," I said. "Look at her photo again."

I held up my P-tab to the woman, but she barely gave it a glance. "Yes, that's her. I'm sorry she died in that fire, it really was a terrible business. But it was a long time ago."

She stepped inside the factory and closed the door before I could react.

"No, wait!" I called out. But she was gone.

The door wasn't locked, I could have gone inside. I could have screamed and shouted and demanded to know the truth about my mother.

But, for the first time in my life, I was afraid of what I might hear. The memory of her, distant and fragile though it was, had been a constant comfort throughout my life. How dare this stranger take that small precious thing and crush it under her shoe.

I sat down on the dirty ground in front of the clothing factory and I'm not ashamed to say that there were tears in my eyes. All the strength had gone out of my body. It was like it was the whole of me, not just my memories, that had been crushed under the heel of the old, bitter woman.

The door opened behind me and I was startled to my feet. I turned, expecting to see one of the workers come out.

But it was the manager again. She still had that severe expression, but within it was a crack of conciliation. "Hey, Isabette's child!"

she called. "Seeing as you're here, you can do me a favour."

I stared at her; trying to reconcile her dismissive attitude with this new request.

"For the Deity's sake, it's not a bad thing," she said. "Your mother left a box of bits and pieces here when she died. I never figured out what to do with it and it's still taking up space in my loft. If you want to take it away, I can have my space back."

"Yes," I said, wiping my eyes. "Yes, please."

She led me inside the factory. It was a vast shed full of people and machinery, sewing and cutting and laying out patterns onto cloth. At the far end, I thought I saw a group of people standing around watching, but when I looked harder they turned out to be mannequins with blank faces wearing selections of half-finished clothing.

To the side was a set of narrow metal stairs which led to a mezzanine floor. The manager walked up them with heavy, clonking footsteps. I followed in my softer-stepping boots with anticipation and dread at what 'a box of bits and pieces' could mean.

At the top of the stairs, a series of closed rooms – offices, or individual workrooms I imagined – lay down one side of a single corridor. The manager passed straight by them all to a second, narrower and steeper set of stairs.

She led me up those stairs into one large room at the top with a low ceiling barely higher than my head. The manager had called it a loft, but most people would have called it a junk room. It was literally full of bags and boxes stacked haphazardly on top of each other. The jumble was presided over by two naked and bashed mannequins; one with an arm missing, the other with a hole where its right eye should be. Rolls of fabric leant against one of the walls and beside them was a rack of drawers, some with oddments of thread spilling out.

"Now," said the manager, placing her hands on her hips. "If only I can find it. It's been years since I've seen it." She waded into the mess and started moving boxes and tipping over bags with all the diligence of a beggar scrabbling around for scraps in someone else's rubbish.

I took a step forward and stood on something squashy, which turned out to be a ball of wool. There were very few places to step that didn't involve treading on something. But, behind me, there was a box that looked sturdy enough, so I picked my way through the detritus and sat tentatively on it. Fortunately, it held my weight.

"So you knew my mother?" I said, emboldened by the fact that she'd taken me inside.

"I did," said the manager as she lifted a box on her left and dumped it down on her right so a cloud of dust flew up in her face.

"This might sound a stupid question," I said. "But did she have anything to do with the royal family? Someone told me she might have been one of the staff at Londos House, except I thought she worked here."

The manager stared at me down the length of the junk room and wiped back a few strands of grey hair which had worked their way loose from her ponytail. "Of course she worked for the royal family."

"Didn't she work here?"

"We had a royal commission back then. We did all the clothes for the Queen, the King and the little princes. Did you seriously not know?"

"No."

The manager moved another bag out of the way and it fell over, causing scraps of fabric to spill out onto the pile where she'd dumped it. "She was the King's favourite. She made all his clothes eventually."

I relaxed a little more. That explained the picture. The King had been wearing a handsome suit in the picture and was showing it off, with the woman who had made it for him.

"I shouldn't have let it continue, to be truthful," said the manager. "But I had a softer heart in those days."

"What do you mean?"

She ignored my question. Deliberately so, it seemed. "I swear the box was over here somewhere. I keep saying I'll have a sort out when we have a quiet period, but the orders either pick up again or some of the staff leave and there's no one to spare." She stood up straight, put her hands on her hips and looked around. "Hang on… This might be it…"

She waded into the far corner by the mannequins, moved a roll of fabric and yet another bag, in order to get to a box behind. It looked identical to the others, but this time she didn't dump it out of the way, she carried it and brought it over to me.

I stood to receive the gift which she dropped at my feet. The box was sealed and had one word written in joined up writing with a circle around it at the top left-hand corner: 'Isabette'.

I squatted down and touched the box. It was the only thing of my mother's that I had ever touched as an adult. All her possessions had perished along with her in the fire. Or so I thought.

"What did you mean earlier when you said you should have sacked her?" I asked.

"I'm sorry, I thought you knew."

"Knew what?"

"That she was his favourite."

"The King?" I asked.

She didn't answer. She seemed reluctant.

"Please," I said. "I need to know. She was my mother."

The woman was breathing a little heavy having moved all those boxes around. She took a step past me and sat down where I had been sitting moments before. "Your mother was part of the team at the beginning," she said. "We were commissioned to make all the clothing for the royal household, as I said. But King John came to request her personally. For a man, even a rich one, he had a lot of clothes made and requested a lot of alterations. I began to suspect it wasn't really the clothes that he wanted, if you see what I mean."

"I don't see what you mean," I said. Except I was afraid I did know exactly what she was implying and it was making me feel sick. I reached out a hand to steady myself.

"I shouldn't have let it continue. But after the hell of the plague, we all needed a little bit of comfort, if you see what I mean. Not that the Queen thought so. She cancelled the commission eventually – bye bye golden ticket."

"Are you saying…?" I swallowed. "My mother was the King's mistress?"

"I'm not saying anything." She bent down – almost pushing me out of the way – and picked up the box. "It was only gossip."

She carried the box with purposeful strides back to the stairs. I followed, barely able to breathe the air which felt like it had been sucked out of the room.

"What are the dates?" I said, hurrying after her as best I could down the stairs.

She wasn't listening. She kept walking.

Along the corridor. Down the first set of steps and out into the street.

She dumped the box unceremoniously outside the door.

Breathless, confused and scared, I stood between her and the door so she could not get past me.

"Tell me about the dates," I said.

The woman frowned. "I don't remember exactly. But it had to have been after the plague because that's what killed off King Alfred. We worked flat out when the Queen announced she was going to marry John Aberchan. She wanted everyone in the royal household to have special clothing for the great alliance between Fertilla's greatest families: 'to celebrate a union to save the planet' and all that drakh. So, yeah, Isabette would have first met King John soon after the plague. I think she even made his wedding suit. You can work out the dates yourself."

I was trying to work them out. I was trying desperately and not wanting to believe what my calculations were telling me could be possible.

"If you'll excuse me," said the manager. "I have work to do."

She walked around me and opened the door to the factory.

"Just one bit of advice," she said before she went in. "Don't even think about trying to claim any inheritance. Take it from me, you're better off staying well away from that royal family."

But her words were no more than noise fluttering above the storm of thoughts in my head.

A relationship no one had told me about. A photograph hidden in royal archives. A note on my file by a man who shouldn't have cared about me.

I didn't want to think it. But once the thought had started to form, I could not stop it.

Chapter Fourteen

I HAD TO GET out of Londos, I had to get away from Mandi's house and I had to get away from Stephen. With still no message from Nick, I had no reason to stay.

Freddi's invitation to visit his daughter's farm was still open and so that's where I went. The farm lay some distance outside of Londos and the rumble of the transport across the dusty plains of Fertilla soothed my troubled mind until I was able to let it go numb. For someone who is used to travelling across light years of space, it was all too short a journey and I was soon at my destination and being greeted by Freddi and his two daughters.

Angelina and Janelle, or Ange and Jan as they introduced themselves, were older than me by ten years or more. It struck me, as it had done the first time I'd met them, how it underlined the age difference between Freddi and me. It is, perhaps, one of the reasons why I look up to him so much – not that I would actually admit it in front of him.

Most of their farm was one vast agro-dome where they grew their crops and reared livestock, with one area set aside as their home. This was an enclosure built onto the planet's surface, much like the one which formed Londos, except much smaller and containing only the single dwelling, quaintly called 'the farmhouse'.

I was shown to a small, but immaculately kept bedroom upstairs where I dumped my overnight bag, and then down to a large communal space they referred to as the 'living room'. It had a mix-match of old and sagging sofas and armchairs around the outside and a large dining table with sufficient chairs for six people in the middle. At busier times of the farming year, I was told that farm labourers would gather there for a meal before bedding down for the night on site in order to get a good start first thing in the morning.

The women said they were preparing a special meal for us and went off into the kitchen, leaving me and Freddi sitting next to each other on a saggy sofa.

"Your daughters look well," I commented.

"They are," said Freddi.

"It must be good to see them again."

"In a manner of speaking. It's family. You know how that is."

"Yes," I said, even though I didn't really.

"Are you going to tell me what's on your mind, Cassy?"

"I don't know what you mean."

"There has to be a reason you came all the way out here when you told me you had stuff to do in Londos."

"You invited me. Does there have to be another reason?"

"For most people, no. For you, yes."

We had spent too many years travelling through the galaxy together for me to hide anything from him. Not that I wanted to. I wanted to talk to him about it – I *needed* to talk to him about it – but it was all so messed up in my head. So I let it spill out of me in a jumble as chaotic and upside down as the store room at the top of the clothing factory where my mother used to work.

Freddi raised his eyebrows. "You think King John could be your father?"

I sighed and flopped back on the saggy sofa. "I don't know. The dates mean it's possible – I've never known when my birthday actually is."

"You tell people you don't know when your birthday is so you don't have to celebrate it."

"Just because it's convenient doesn't mean it's not true," I pointed out. "I assumed no one knew when I was born because record keeping was so bad after the plague, and no one could ask my mother because she was dead. But what if the date was kept vague because the man I thought was my father wasn't my father after all?"

"That's a bit of conclusion to jump to."

"It's the same conclusion the clothing factory manager jumped to – except I don't think she had to do much jumping."

"Okay, let's imagine it's true," said Freddi. "Let's imagine your mother was the King's mistress, you were conceived after your father died and the dates were fudged to hide the fact. Why would Prince Stephen show you that photograph? The last thing the royal family needs is a scandal involving a common freelancer."

"*Common?* Thanks!"

"You know what I mean, Cassy."

"I don't think he knows. Stephen said he didn't really know his father."

"Oh *Stephen* now, is it?"

I gave him a hard stare. "Don't look at me in that tone of voice," I said, mixing my metaphors on purpose. "You didn't hear the way the clothing manager spoke to me. You didn't see the way she looked at me."

"I still say it's gossip and speculation."

"Then how do you explain the photograph?"

"As you said, the King had a new set of clothes and he was having his picture taken with the woman who made them for him. And, for some reason, a dog."

"Maybe," I said, uncertainly.

"Is it beyond the realms of possibility that he was doing your mother a favour? I mean, it's like I'm doing you a favour by inviting you to stay here – it doesn't mean I'm sleeping with you."

At the point he said the words, '*I'm sleeping with you*', the door opened and Ange, the older one of Freddi's daughters, came in carrying two plates of food. Life had been kinder to her features, I noticed, than it had been to Freddi's, but the family resemblance was still there.

"Do you want to sit up at the table?" said Ange, placing the plates down on the two settings nearest to us. "Before it gets cold."

Jan followed her sister into the room, also carrying two plates of food. By this time, the smell had started to percolate and I could pick out the aroma of onions, tomatoes and, I was fairly sure, meat.

Stew was usually an excuse to throw any old thing resembling food into a pot and boil it until it was all the same colour and no one could really tell what was in it. But Freddi's daughters' version of stew had an actual colour to it. It was a glistening reddy brown as opposed to a sludgy muddy brown, with identifiable pieces of vegetables and several chunks of meat which were big enough to bite on as opposed to swallow without noticing like many other 'meat' stews I had been served. What's more, the fat of the meat had melted into the gravy, giving the whole meal a flavour that caused my stomach to gurgle with delight.

Such was the privilege of living on a farm.

For a moment, the only sound around the table was the clinking of spoons on bowls as we began to eat.

It was Ange who took it upon herself to start the small talk. "Tell me, Cassy, what's Dad like when he's on board a spaceship?"

I finished my mouthful of stew. "Indispensable," I said. "He knows every bit of that ship. He can fly it, he can fix it, he has a kind of sixth sense as to things like what supplies we need."

"We could do with someone like that around the farm," said Jan.

Ange made a not so subtle attempt to kick her sister under the table. All three of them looked down at their stew and avoided eye contact.

"So," I said, breaking the awkward silence. "What's happening on the farm at the moment?"

"We're preparing for harvest. Things are going to get busy here soon," said Ange.

"Except one of the machines is broken," said Jan.

"That reminds me," said Freddi. "I was going to have a look at it for you."

"No need," said Jan.

"I can do it after dinner if you like."

"I said, no need. I've called the maintenance firm, they'll be here in the morning."

"You didn't have to do that, Jan. I said I would take a look. I forgot, that's all."

The tension closed in around the table and, for a while, the only sound was the clatter of spoons on bowls and the distinct absence of conversation.

Ange looked up from her stew and gave me a smile. Making a deliberate effort again. "Dad tells me you were born on Fertilla."

"That's right."

"You weren't a spacefarer to start with, then?"

"No, but I dreamt of going into space. I didn't feel there was anything keeping me on Fertilla."

"A bit like Dad, then," said Jan.

Freddi shot her a warning look. "Janelle!"

"It's true, isn't it, Dad?"

"Do we have to talk about this now?" he said, glancing over at me. "My friend is here."

"Oh your friend is here! Well I'm sorry, but when else are we going to talk about it? You're always in space."

I felt I was intruding on something private. Like I had inadvertently walked out of a maintenance door of a town enclosure and was struggling with breathing the planet's natural air. "Maybe I should go up to my room," I suggested.

"No, it's fine," Ange insisted, gesturing that I should stay in my seat. "Finish your stew."

I looked down at my empty bowl. I had already finished.

"I went into space to help you," said Freddi. "Both you and Angelina, you know that."

"You went into space," said Jan. "Because Mum died and you couldn't stay here and face your grief."

"I sent you back everything I earned," said Freddi.

"Maybe we didn't want your money. Maybe we wanted our dad."

Freddi was shaking now. At first, I thought, with anger. But then I realised he was upset. "I'm going to go outside for a bit," he said, keeping his voice low as he tried to keep the emotion out of it.

He stood from the table and turned away from his two daughters.

I watched him go, debating with myself whether I should stay and be polite or go after my friend.

From the moment I thought it, I realised my friend would win the debate every time.

I stood up. "Thank you for the stew," I said and hurried after him.

Stepping into the vastness of an agro-dome with only a thin, transparent membrane to protect me from the natural atmosphere of the planet could be frightening. At least, for someone who had grown up in a town with no sky and constrained by an enclosure no taller than a three-storey building. I had visited agro-domes before, but not for many years, and so I hesitated before operating the door which led out of the farmhouse.

The locks disengaged and the airtight seal decoupled with a hiss. The barrier opened and daylight from Fertilla's sun fell onto my face. I felt its subtle warmth on my cheeks as I blinked into its brightness and looked out onto a landscape which seemed to stretch to infinity. Above me – the height of three Londos-sized enclosures – was the delicate shield of the dome itself and, beyond that, the soft pink of the Fertillan sky reaching up until it touched space.

As I overcame my primal urge to run back into the confines of the building, I was able to look around and take in the sights, sounds and smells of life thriving all around me. Grass as tall as my hip nodded heavy with grain to my left. A carpet of green from a crop that could have been cabbages rolled out to the right. In front were the delicate yellow flowers of a crop I didn't recognise. The smell was amazing. It had a freshness that the recycled air of places like Londos could never replicate. Each carbon dioxide breath I exhaled was absorbed by the plants and converted into oxygen which they released back into the air along with their pollen. I could smell its sweetness nestled among the earthy undertones given off by the excretions of animals whose eerie bellows and bleats I heard in the distance.

A dark figure stood against the yellow of the field in front of me. It was Freddi, his outline distinguishable by the way he leant his weight over to one side to favour his good leg.

I took a tentative step forward, leaving the sanctity of the doorway for the vast expanse of the dome. I paused to allow my senses to catch up with what my conscious mind was trying to tell them: it was perfectly safe.

Approaching Freddi, allowing my boots to crunch on the grit of the dirt beneath so he could hear me coming, I saw him bring his hand up to his face to wipe what I imagined were tears that had fallen onto his cheeks.

"I'm sorry you had to hear that," he said.

"There's nothing to be sorry about."

"They're right, though. I did abandon them."

"You needed to earn money," I said, repeating what he had told me the one time we had talked about it.

"That's what I told myself."

I took a deep breath of the sweet, fresh air. "But look at what they've done. The farm is thriving."

"I'm proud of my girls. When Ellen died, I couldn't have imagined it ever looking like this again."

"Must have been tough," I said.

"We lost more or less everything in the plague. Crops were left to die or go to seed. I tried to encourage workers to come here, but they were either sick themselves or were scared of getting sick. Once Ellen got ill, of course, we were in quarantine. I did what I could, but between nursing her and trying to keep the animals alive, it was a losing battle. I think I went to pieces a bit when Ellen didn't make it. That's when Ange and Jan mostly took over running the place. I'd hoped once the quarantine was lifted, the workers would return and we'd make a go of it, but the population of Fertilla had been decimated and outsiders didn't want to come to a plague planet. Not for the wages we were offering."

"Is that when you signed up with the pirates?"

He nodded. "I could earn more money in space than I ever could under an agro-dome. I worked hard, sent money back and prayed it would be enough to get the farm back on its feet again."

"You did the right thing."

"Did I? Or was it an excuse to run away from the memory of Ellen? I mean, look at Ange and Jan now: grown women who've worked so hard they haven't had time for husbands – or wives for that matter, I wouldn't mind. They haven't had time for children. I should be a grandfather by now."

I put a friendly arm around his shoulder. "You look too young to be a grandfather."

"You're a good liar, Cassy."

"I'm really not," I said. "There's still time for Ange and Jan. Perhaps I could increase your wages a little bit so you can send a bit more home and they can employ a farm manager or something."

"If you can afford it," said Freddi. "We haven't picked up another job and we've got all those repairs to pay for."

"We'll get work. It'll be fine."

He sniffed and wiped his nose on the back of his hand. "Talking of husbands, what about you and the prince?"

I felt my cheeks redden, and not because of the heat of the sun. "There is no me and the prince."

"Would you like there to be?"

"Freddi! I just told you he could be my brother."

"How do you know if you haven't done a DNA test?"

"I can't turn up at Londos House with a swab kit and ask the prince for a sample!"

"Obviously!" Freddi rolled his eyes like I was being ridiculous. "You need to be a bit more subtle than that. If I hadn't cleared up after the pair of *you* drank all *my* beer on the ship, we could have used the saliva on his glass. Maybe he'll invite you around for tea again and you could steal his cup."

"Because getting arrested for theft from the royal household is really going to help," I said, sarcastically.

"Then you need to ask him. If you don't find out the truth, Cassy, you're always going to wonder."

Chapter Fifteen

REDDI WANTED TO leave the farm the next morning. I tried to persuade him to stay, but he said the tension was too intense and all three of them needed space to calm down. I suspected this was what always happened when Freddi returned home to his daughters. The pent-up anger from all those years ago was released and, rather than having a pleasant family reunion, it turned into a massive argument. I wanted to tell him to break the cycle of arguing, leaving, coming back and arguing again, but he wasn't ready to hear it and so I kept quiet.

Mandi had a spare room she was happy to rent to him and so Freddi and I both went to Mandi's house.

As I entered my room, I saw the box of my mother's things where I had left it – still sealed – under my bed. On the corner, I read the word 'Isabette'. Whatever lay inside frightened me. Only five days since I had returned to Fertilla and almost everything I thought I knew about my mother had been called into question.

I took the top sheet off my bed and draped it over the box so I wouldn't have to look at it. I might be cold at night, but at least I could save myself the pain of any further revelations a little while longer.

I LOVE FREDDI. In the special way that shipmates who travel together in space love each other. But he does have the annoying habit of being right a lot of the time.

If I didn't find out the truth about King John's relationship with my mother, then I would always be wondering. The key to that truth lay with Prince Stephen. Either with what he knew or with what his DNA could tell me. So I sent a note to Courtier Brimble saying that I needed to speak to the prince again.

When I received a reply to say that my request was 'acceptable to His Royal Highness', I felt my heart beat faster. It was a crazy, adolescent feeling of excitement that couldn't be the sort of love a sister has for a brother. Or maybe my body was craving the affections of any man, having been denied them so long, that it didn't really care what was in his DNA, as long as it had a Y chromosome.

I presented myself at Londos House on the day and time stated in the reply and Brimble showed me into the same ornate room where we had had tea. Stephen was reclining on the sofa with a P-tab held up to his face and his booted feet up on the shiny, and doubtless expensive, table. I swear I saw a flicker of disapproval pass across the courtier's face before he hid it under his mask of servitude.

"Individual Sesaan Cassandra, Sire," Brimble announced.

Stephen tapped something on the tab and dropped it onto the table. As he stood up, I saw he was wearing the same waistcoat as last time, but had chosen a blue shirt to go with it. He had kept the top two buttons undone, allowing a few dark hairs from his chest to appear from beneath the fabric. Before I could stop myself, I thought about touching his chest and teasing those strands of hair with my fingers. I cursed my hormones. They were working overtime and I needed to think clearly.

Brimble was staring at me and I realised I had forgotten to curtsey. Hurriedly and clumsily, I crossed one foot in front of the other, bent my knees and bowed my head.

Stephen dismissed the courtier and, as Brimble closed the door behind me, I heard Stephen chuckling. He took my hand and pulled me up to standing straight.

"You look funny when you do that," he said.

"Do I?"

"Yes, but it's fine."

"I'm sorry. It's not the sort of thing I normally have to do on a spaceship."

"I'm sure it isn't." He chuckled again. "But no need to apologise, I quite like it."

I was about to ask him the thing that I had come to ask him, but he interrupted my thoughts before I could find the right words.

"Do you want to see something cool?" he said.

"Um…" I was still trying to think of the right way to phrase my question. "Depends what it is."

"You see, other people would have just said 'yes, Sire' whether they wanted to or not."

"Is that what I should have said?" I was embarrassed and beginning to realise my upbringing in an orphans' home had in no way prepared me for socialising with royalty. Even if it turned out there was some royal blood inside of me.

"I prefer that you say whatever you feel like saying," said the prince. "But, don't worry, it's a nice cool thing, not a scary cool thing. At least, I think it's nice. This way."

He took my hand again and led me to a door at the back of the room. Then we were hurrying down a corridor like excited children. Well, he seemed excited, I was nervous.

He let go of my hand as we turned a corner and entered another corridor. There was a member of the Fertillan Guard coming the opposite way. She stopped when she saw the prince and bowed her head.

"Sire," she acknowledged.

Stephen carried on like he hadn't even noticed she was there.

When he reached a door at the end of the corridor he stopped and turned to me with an excited grin. "Ready?"

"I think so."

How was it possible to be ready for something when I had no idea what it was?

He placed a hand on a lockpad beside the door and there was the click of bolts followed by the hiss of an airtight seal, just like on Freddi's daughters' farm. The door swung open and a blaze of warm, natural light touched my body. I gasped as I realised I was standing on the threshold between Londos and the surface of Fertilla.

But I was still breathing.

I was protected by a transparent bubble, like an agro-dome, but only the size of a small room. A dome filled, not with crops, but with an ordinary solid floor and soft furnishings.

"We call it The Conservatory," said Stephen. "You can come in, it's okay."

He went in first and took my hand to encourage me to follow.

The room was a window on Fertilla. Beyond the see-through barrier, the dusty reddish yellow crust of earth stretched out so far that it appeared to fall off the edge into the sun. The sun itself was like the brightest lamp it was possible to imagine, but ten times brighter. It hurt to look at it.

"The original people who built Londos House put this in. Isn't it cool?"

"It's amazing." I started to breathe again as my mind adjusted to still being inside, even if what my eyes were showing me was the planet's surface. Beyond the dome, to one side, was a metal mound that rose out of the ground and stretched as far as I could see until it touched the soft pink of the sky.

"Is that Londos town?" I said.

"Yes. And over there, you can just about see some agro-domes."

He was right. At the edge of Londos, the white bubbles of enclosed agricultural land glinted in the sunlight. It was just possible to see a hint of green from the crops growing inside.

"It's amazing," I said again.

"When I stand here and look out, I sometimes imagine what it must have been like for the first humans who landed here and stepped out in their spacesuits. It's hard for us who've lived on an agricultural planet all our lives and walked through the richness of our farms to understand why they were excited. To us, the natural planet seems inhospitable, but look–"

Stephen pointed to the ground outside. At first, I saw nothing but the dusty earth. Until I looked at the exact spot where he was pointing: a scraggy brown plant had somehow pulled itself out of the ground and was growing on the planet's surface. Without any protection of an agro-dome or help from a human. And once I had seen one, I began to see more. Small, but resilient plants scattered around and somehow managing to survive.

"That's why they were excited," said Stephen. "If plants could live here, then maybe we could live here too. Those people who had fled the Oblivion War and made it out here to the Rim must have travelled to many dead worlds and barely inhabitable regions of space. Then they came here and found things were growing, so they called the planet Fertilla."

I looked out again at the planet's surface and it seemed even more beautiful.

The sound of someone else coming in through the door interrupted my thoughts. His wheezy breath told me it was Brimble even before I turned to see he was carrying a tea tray.

"Excuse me, Sire," he said. "Your tea, Sire."

"Excellent, Brimble!" said Stephen. "Put it on the table, would you?"

In the middle of the room was another one of those calf-height tables, except this one was not much bigger than the tray itself.

Brimble put the tray down, nodded an acknowledgement to me and bowed to the prince. "Thank you, Sire," he said and left.

I couldn't imagine spending my life saying, 'yes, Sire' all the time like him. It was easier to imagine stepping out onto the planet for the first time in a spacesuit.

"I assume you like tea?" said Stephen. "You drank it last time."

"Yes," I said. "I like tea. Especially the honey."

"I only ask because we used to serve tea to one of the admin staff who would come over to meetings and he always drank it without saying anything. Years later it turned out he hated the stuff and was only drinking it to be polite. What is it with some people?"

"I think they might be intimidated because you are a prince," I said.

"I think they might be too."

For a moment, I thought he was going to say something else, but instead he turned away from me and looked down at the tray. "I imagine the tea will be brewed now."

He sat down on one of the soft chairs beside the table and poured a cup for each of us. I sat in a chair on the other side of the table. It was not as plush as the sofa where we had first sat and drunk tea. The chair had hard arm rests and thinner cushions, but was comfortable enough. And the view was amazing.

"What was it you wanted to say to me?" he asked, picking up his tea and blowing some of the steam off its hot surface.

I squirmed in my seat. I was hoping to find the right moment, not have it sprung upon me like that.

"The note you sent to Brimble said you wanted to see me about something," Stephen prompted.

"Yes." I took a breath. I thought about picking up my tea to give me a moment to gather my thoughts, but I was too nervous and I thought I might spill it. "I spoke to someone who used to work with my mother. She was a seamstress, you know."

"That's what it says in your file," said Stephen, sipping his tea.

"Yes." Of course he knew that. "Well, it turns out, the place where she worked used to make all the clothes for the royal household and my mother made clothes for your father."

"That explains it!" said Stephen. "That's why he's standing like that in the picture; he's showing off his new clothes. Next to the person who made them."

"That's what I thought," I said.

Except that's not what I thought. That's not what I thought at all.

"Is there something else, Cassy?"

"I don't want to say anything bad about your father," I said.

"It's not something that hasn't already been said, I'm sure. I hear the staff talking sometimes. They think I'm not listening, but sometimes I can't help it."

I took another breath. "The person I talked to said my mother made a lot of clothes for your father. She said she came up to Londos House a lot. More than might be expected for a seamstress."

I said no more. I let Stephen join the dots like I had done a couple of days ago.

"You think they might have been having a relationship?"

"It's not me who thinks it," I said quickly. "It's the colleague of my mother's."

"Would it matter if they had?"

It was a strange question. "No," I said, really meaning yes. "It's just that I've looked at the dates, and what with your father giving me protected status and everything…"

"You think…?" Stephen laughed. Laughed so loud it echoed inside the dome above us. "You think my father could also be your father? No no, Cassy. Really, he can't be."

I felt myself go red. "Like I said, I don't want to say anything bad about your father."

"My dear, Cassy. It's impossible, believe me."

"How can you know for sure?" I said. "The dates…"

Stephen stood and came over to where I was sitting. My body tensed; a little scared at what he might do.

He took my hand – like he had done when I had curtsied before him – and drew me up to standing.

"This is how sure I am that you and I do not have the same father." He leant forward and kissed my lips.

Fire erupted inside of me; hotter than the Fertillan sun. His hands cupped my face and drew me closer. I allowed myself to sink into him as my mouth joined with his mouth and I breathed in the scent of him.

The noise of the door opening broke us apart. Stephen seemed almost to jump back from me as he turned to see Brimble enter.

I was breathing heavily and I'm sure I was flushed. But if Brimble noticed, he didn't let it show.

"Excuse me, Sire," he said. "But Prince James is here."

"Drakh!" said Stephen.

"You asked me to let you know, Sire."

"Yes, Brimble, thank you. I lost track of time, that's all." He turned to me. "It's my brother. I have business to attend to, I'm sorry."

"No need to apologise," I said, realising I was repeating exactly what he had said to me earlier.

"But I'll see you again?" he said.

"I don't know…" How does a freelancer keep seeing a prince when she has no official royal business?

"Are you coming to the funeral?"

"Funeral?"

"Andrus Hoggard's funeral is tomorrow. You were with him during the last few days of his life, it wouldn't be inappropriate."

"I suppose I could come," I said.

"That's arranged then. Brimble can give you the details." He turned to his servant. "Where's James now?"

"In your office, Sire."

As the two of them talked with their back to me, I reached down with my shirt sleeve pulled over my hand and picked up Stephen's teacup. I slipped the cup – although it was somewhat large – into the inside pocket of the bulky jacket I had worn specially. There was still some tea in the bottom of the cup and I tried to keep my face passive as I felt the liquid, which had gone cold, run down my side.

Stephen headed off to his office to meet with his brother, leaving Brimble to show me out.

To reach the entrance of Londos House, we went down a set of different and less elaborate corridors, which were probably used mostly by servants.

When we arrived, Brimble asked, "Will we be seeing more of you?"

"I really don't know," I told him. "Possibly."

"Then you won't be needing a souvenir of your visit," he said. He held out his hand like a teacher demanding a toy off a naughty child.

I sighed. So I hadn't been clandestine in taking the cup at all. I reached into my inside jacket pocket and retrieved it for him.

"Thank you, Individual Cassandra." He took the cup from me. "See you again."

He went back inside Londos House, leaving me to walk out onto the street without the DNA sample I had intended to collect.

CHAPTER SIXTEEN

CHECKED MY MESSAGES when I got back and there was, at last, one from Nick.

He said he had decrypted Hoggard's code and I could come to collect it at his workshop in the evening after he'd finished for the day.

Freddi tagged along.

"I thought Londos was supposed to be full of people," he observed as we walked through the streets approaching Nick's workshop.

It was quieter, and later, than the first time I had been there. "People like to go home after work," I said.

"Townsfolk are strange," said Freddi.

I laughed. "Why do you think I like spaceships?"

I pushed at Nick's door like the first time I had been there, expecting it to be open, but it didn't move. It was not only closed, but locked. There were no sounds of music or slightly out of tune singing. There were no sounds of movement inside at all. I wondered if Nick had gone home and forgotten about us.

I knocked on the door and waited.

Moments later, I heard the sound of someone coming down the stairs. Nick opened the door and paused on the doorstep.

"Who's this?" he said, looking at Freddi.

"It's my shipmate, Freddi," I said. "He's staying with me in Londos for a while. That's okay, isn't it?"

Nick didn't say whether it was or whether it wasn't, he just ushered us inside. Once we were in, he closed and locked the door behind us. He pushed past us and rushed back up to his workshop.

When I joined him moments later, I saw it looked more or less the same as the first time. It was still a mess, only some of the mess had been moved around a little. There were a few more abandoned drinking cups and one dinner plate with the remains of the meal it once contained congealed into an unhealthy-looking smear.

Nick leant back on his workbench with his hands in his pockets. "What exactly did you mean when you asked me to do this job 'off the books'?"

"Just that the code was given to me by a friend and he asked me to look after it." It was only a half-lie. Maybe not even that, maybe a quarter of one.

"It wasn't because it was stolen?"

He was starting to make me feel uneasy, but I tried to hide it and be casual. "What makes you say that?"

"The watermark running through the whole thing saying authorised eyes only."

"You de-coded it?" I said.

Nick allowed himself a smug grin. "I said I did, didn't I?"

He took his hands out of his pockets and walked around the other side of the workbench to his computer equipment. "It was a sophisticated encryption," he said. "But an old one, and there exists decryption software for it if you know where to look. Which, fortunately, I do."

"What does it say?" said Freddi.

"Apart from authorised eyes only?" said Nick.

"Apart from that."

"A lot of scientific gobbledygook."

"Can I see?" said Freddi.

"I don't see why not."

Freddi made his way to Nick's bench, carefully stepping over several bits of mess on the floor as he did so. Not to be left out, I followed.

Nick awoke the main screen in front of him with a tap and its bluey-whiteness shone out across us. "It didn't make any sense to me at first," he said. "I thought I was using the wrong software or maybe it was double code – when someone wants to make something extra secure, they encrypt it twice – or more, sometimes."

He tapped the screen again and writing appeared. But not writing like I understood it. It was one long, unbroken nonsense word that filled the screen in block capitals.

"Then I looked at it closer," said Nick. "And I realised the code was made up of the same four letters: A, T, C, G. There's only one thing that produces a code like that."

"The Deity," said Freddi.

"I was going to say nature," said Nick. "But, yeah."

I looked at the screen again. He was right. The sequence began at the top of the screen, ATGCTAGCTAACT… and continued on like that in what appeared, to me, to be a random pattern until it reached the bottom of the screen. "It's a genetic code?" I said.

"A big long DNA sequence," said Nick. "What it's for, I don't know."

He scrolled down and the letters kept coming, pages and pages of them. "After that, the decryption software starting pulling out other stuff. Stuff that looked like an accompanying scientific paper. I read a bit of it, but it went over my head. Then I figured I better stop reading it."

The genetic sequence disappeared off the top of the screen and was replaced by writing that I could actually read. Dense paragraphs interspersed with labelled diagrams and, underneath them, in large faint letters written at a forty-five degree angle, the words: AUTHORISED EYES ONLY.

"Authorised by who?" I wondered out loud.

"I don't know, but I would say someone who was worried about the information getting out," said Nick.

He tapped the screen again to bring up another page. This time, it was a single paragraph in bold, plain language:

All materials are strictly for authorised personnel only. Not to be removed from this laboratory, copied or shared with anyone. The contents of this document must not be discussed in any way. Personnel are reminded of the sensitive nature of these documents and the risks associated with allowing their contents to be known outside of those with the appropriate clearance.

Freddi peered closer at the screen. "Would you mind if I…?"

Nick took a step back and Freddi moved in, scrolling through to bring up page after page of the scientific document. As much gobbledygook to me as Nick claimed it was to him.

"Who, exactly, was this 'friend' of yours who had the code?" said Nick, turning to glare at me.

"Someone on my ship," I said. "They left the code behind, I told you."

"It doesn't look like the sort of thing someone would leave lying around on a freelancer's ship."

"I think the man who left it was in a hurry," I said.

Nick's eyes narrowed. "What sort of hurry?"

I winced as I told him. "The sort that had the Fertillan Guard after him."

"So this document…?"

"I think you're right, I think he stole it."

Nick's face hardened with anger. "And you decided not to mention this when you brought it to my workshop?"

"I hoped I could get it de-coded quietly. I hoped I'd find out what it was and no one else would need to know."

"You're damned right no one else is going to know." Nick pushed Freddi out of the way of his screen. He tapped it and the image of the document disappeared in front of us. He kept tapping and I saw the word, 'delete' appear briefly before it, too, disappeared.

"Hey, what are you doing?" I stepped forward, but Nick pushed me back.

"Making sure there's no evidence of this document left on my equipment."

"That 'authorised personnel' stuff doesn't really mean anything,"

I said. "People put that on important papers just to scare other people."

"Works, doesn't it?" said Nick. Another piece of the scientific paper appeared on the screen and abruptly vanished as the word 'delete' flashed in front of our eyes.

"I don't understand why you asked me here if all you were going to do was delete the code."

He turned to me again. Behind him, the blank screen cast its empty bluey-white light. "Why did you bring this to me?" he asked. "Why did you simply not return it to your friend?"

"He died," I said.

Nick nodded, like he wasn't surprised. "How did he die?"

"Not in a good way."

"That's what I thought."

He turned back to his workbench and hit a button underneath. A drawer slid open and revealed the memory ball sitting in a little holder. Freddi reached for it, but Nick snatched it up ahead of him. "I put everything on the ball: the original code and the decrypted version."

I sighed with relief. He hadn't deleted it after all. At least, not entirely.

"You can take it away as long as you promise not to come back," he said.

"Absolutely. I promise." I opened my palm and he dropped the ball into it. It was warm from being inside the equipment. "I still need to pay you."

"No you don't. No money changes hands; nothing is traceable." He looked tense, pale, agitated. "Make sure you delete all data linking us on your devices. Messages, appointments, everything."

"You're really worried," I said.

"I've got kids now," was all he said.

Freddi pulled at my arm. "Come on, Cassy, let's go."

I gripped the memory ball tight in my fist and nodded an acknowledgement to Nick. "Thanks for this," I said.

Freddi tugged at my arm again and I allowed myself to be led to the door.

We had to wait for Nick at the bottom of the stairs because he had locked us in. He said nothing when he came down. He opened the door, we stepped out onto the street, he slammed it shut behind us and I heard the locks click into place.

I started to walk away, but Freddi pulled me to one side. "I think I know what the code is," he whispered.

"You do?"

"Let's not talk here."

Chapter Seventeen

FREDDI SAT HIMSELF down on the bed in my room in Mandi's house. It left me with the one hard, and slightly wonky, chair in the room.

"Do you realise that document shouldn't exist?" he said.

"It nearly didn't. I thought Nick was going to delete the lot." I pressed my hand to my trouser pocket and felt the reassuring hard, round presence of the memory ball.

"It *never* should have existed," said Freddi. "The science in it shouldn't be possible."

"When did you become a budding scientist?" I said.

"I didn't, but I know farming and I saw enough in that document to tell it was research into growing crops. I think Nick saw it too, but he didn't want to admit it to himself."

"Hoggard stole research about growing crops? Why would he risk his life for that? Who would kill for that?"

"If I'm right – and, as you point out, I'm no scientist – lots of people."

I shook my head and the chair wobbled beneath me. None of this seemed relevant, or important. "Freddi, you're going to have to spell this out in words of one syllable."

He sighed and ran his hands through his grey and ginger hair. "Fertilla has to be the stupidest name ever for a planet like this. This planet isn't fertile. The earth is dust, oxygen levels are negligible, it hardly ever rains, the sun is too far away to be hot enough and yet there's not the atmosphere to protect us from solar radiation…"

"I get the point," I said. "We had to build agro-domes to grow food. Even I remember that bit from school."

"But there were already plants growing here on the planet's natural surface. That's what gave hope to the original settlers and that's what scientists hoped to capitalise on. But the alien plants are too different from the plants our ancestors brought from SolPrime. You can't stick the two together and grow wheat out on the unprotected Fertillan surface, it doesn't work."

"What about the document?" I said, wishing he would get to the point.

"I think it's a way to make it work. I don't pretend to understand it in detail, but it looked to me like someone has made the impossible possible. They've taken the genetic material from the natural plants on Fertilla and somehow melded it with the DNA of the plants humans brought with them to create a hybrid which doesn't need an agro-dome."

He looked at me with expectation and excitement as he waited for me to understand. I wasn't sure I did. "Why is that important?"

"Oh, Cassy!" said Freddi. He jumped off the bed and paced the room in frustration. "You've spent too much of your life on a spaceship."

"That's a matter of opinion," I said, a little offended.

His pacing brought him back to me and he knelt next to where I was sitting. Totally unexpectedly, he took my hand. I sat back away from him and the chair wobbled. He squeezed my hand tight like he was pressing the information into me, while he kept his voice low so no one might overhear. "Because, Cassy, you could grow such a hybrid plant almost anywhere. Not just outside of an agro-dome on Fertilla, but on other planets with poor soil and weak sunshine. On moons or asteroids where radiation is a problem. On space stations that need to conserve water."

He paused and looked up into my face.

I smiled back; it was making sense. "It's food technology that could be exported across the Rim."

"Yes," he said.

"It could feed people struggling on some of the most inhospitable colonies."

"Yes!" he said.

He let go of my hand and sat back on the floor. He leant against the wardrobe.

I thought about all the many possibilities. I knew nothing about farms, but I had seen the conditions in some of the worst places where people spent their lives worrying about the next meal. "That's got to be worth a lot of money," I said.

Freddi nodded. "Yes."

Chapter Eighteen

A MESSAGE CAME THROUGH from Nanci. She had finished the repairs to our ship and acquired us a new shuttle which she had almost finished fixing. It meant we would be able to leave Fertilla within a couple of days.

I caught Freddi to tell him as he was coming out of the bathroom. His hair was wet from the shower and he had a towel wrapped around the waist of his otherwise naked body.

"I've heard from Nanci," I said, as I stood half in and half out of my room, resting on the frame of the open door.

"And?" he said.

"Almost done. We're more or less ready to leave."

"What about the bill?"

"The bill came with the message. I haven't dared open it yet."

"I can imagine." Freddi took a step towards his room.

"We need to decide what to do," I said.

He paused. "Well, I was going to finish off getting dry and getting dressed, I don't know about you."

I stepped out into the hallway. "We need to decide what we're going to do beyond the next few minutes."

He reached for the door handle. "Do we have to talk about it now?"

"Nanci wants to know when we'll be arriving."

He rolled his eyes. "Fine."

He opened the door, stepped inside and left it open so I could follow him in.

The room, like mine, had been given a Mandi makeover. When I was a child, some of the older boys slept there and, from what I remember from the glimpses I had of it when they went in or out, it was so chaotic it lent a new meaning to the word 'mess'. Now, it was relatively clean and tidy with just the one unmade bed that Freddi had slept in, a wardrobe, and a chair with Freddi's clothes draped across it.

"Close the door, could you?" he said.

I turned around and pushed the door shut. When I turned back, Freddi had whipped the towel off from around his waist and was scrubbing his hair dry with it.

He threw his towel on the bed and reached for his trousers. "What do you *want* to do?" he said.

I threw up my hands in exasperation. I had been asking myself that question all night and got nowhere. "If I knew that, I wouldn't be asking you."

"Oh, so you only consult me when you're stuck, is that it?" he said with a grin.

I gave him a hard stare. "You know what I mean."

While he stepped into his trousers, I went over to his bed, moved the damp towel out of the way and sat myself down on it. It was a cheap bed and bounced several times before I was able to sit still.

Freddi was facing away from me as he did up his trousers and I saw the deep scar across his back that he rarely let me see. It ran all the way from the top of his right shoulder blade down to the bottom of his ribs on the left. I imagined it was a legacy from his pirate days, but he had never told me about it and I hadn't had the audacity to ask him.

"Hoggard said, 'deliver the code,'" I said. "What does that mean? Deliver it where? Deliver it to who?"

Freddi grabbed his shirt from the chair and covered up his scar as he slipped his arms into the sleeves. "Whoever was going to pay him a lot of money to steal it, I would think."

"But he said it was 'our salvation'. Why would he say that if he was doing it for money? He must have known it was technology that could feed the Rim."

"Doesn't mean he wasn't getting paid."

Freddi sat on the chair and did up the buttons of his shirt. I reached into my pocket and pulled out the silver sphere of the memory ball. I held it in my palm. It was small, so apparently insignificant, and yet Hoggard had died for it.

"This thing has caused us nothing but trouble," I said.

"True."

"I was thinking, what if we forget it ever existed? Throw it away, get back to the ship, wormhole off to the Riel system, get a job and go back to how things were."

"You can't throw it away!" said Freddi. "Think what it could mean! Think how many people it could feed."

"It's not worth getting a knife in the back."

"Isn't it?"

"No! Because I would be dead. On the scale of good to bad, dead rates right down there at the bottom of bad, as far as I'm concerned."

"Even if you chuck it in the rubbish, Cassy, you'll still know that you had it. Every time we take on a job and go to a planet where people are struggling to feed themselves, you'll remember what you had in your hand and you'll feel the guilt of what you threw away for a quiet life. Can you live with that?"

"Better than dying with it." I rolled the ball around the palm of my hand.

"Then don't die," said Freddi. "Take it somewhere; give it to someone who will value it and use it."

"We're back to where we started," I said. "Deliver the code to where? Deliver it to who?"

He leant forward on his chair. "It seems to me, you have two choices. You could give it back to the Regellan royal household from where it was apparently stolen – but you've got to ask yourself, if they had food technology which is going to be 'our salvation', why doesn't anyone else know about it? That's, of course, assuming they're going to be grateful and not arrest you. The other choice is to find out where Hoggard was taking it and give it to them in the hope they use it for the good of everyone."

"The second choice is all very well, but you keep forgetting that Hoggard is dead and I can't ask him where he was taking it."

"Isn't it his funeral today?" asked Freddi.

"What were you thinking? That I interrogate his corpse?"

He rolled his eyes. "What I meant is, if there is going to be anywhere you could find someone who knew him, then it's going to be at his funeral. He can't have acted alone. Someone must have known what he was up to, probably even helped him."

I hadn't thought of that. "Asking around without tipping my hand isn't going to be easy," I said.

"Maybe there'll be someone obvious. They give speeches at these things, don't they? There might be a colleague or a friend you could talk to."

"Stephen said he has a widow."

"That's a possibility. I told my wife everything when she was alive."

I shook my head; uncertain. "But Stephen will be there. I said I would meet him. It might be difficult."

"Prince Stephen?"

"Yeah." I looked at the sphere again, mesmerised by its simple, silver beauty.

"Could be an opportunity to sound him out. See if you think you could trust him with the code. Harvest two fields with one machine, as they say."

"I don't know… asking him without asking him also isn't going to be easy."

"Try not to get yourself arrested again, obviously."

I smiled. "Yeah."

"Go to the funeral, Cassy. See what you can find out. If it looks too dangerous, I promise I'll back you whatever you decide. But, as we've come this far, I think you should try."

Chapter Nineteen

The Celebration of Life Chapel described itself as a 'remembrance facility for all faiths and none', which meant if someone died and the people left behind were religious, they held the ceremony there. If someone died and the people left behind didn't want a religious ceremony, it was still held there. The chapel was the only place in Londos licensed to deal with dead bodies. The old human custom of burying people under the ground was banned on Fertilla, partly because it would lead to whole swathes of the planet being turned into graveyards, but mostly because the ground didn't possess the bacteria and soil-dwelling creatures needed to break down a body. Cremation was the only solution, and then in a sealed chamber to prevent ash escaping into the enclosed environment.

I walked over from Mandi's house with Freddi's words still circulating in my mind and the memory ball in my pocket pressing hard against my thigh with each step. Fertillan Guards were patrolling the streets surrounding the chapel and, if that wasn't enough to indicate a royal presence, two of their cars in uniform-brown were parked prominently outside. The chapel entrance was marked by a pair of oversized doors from where a queue of people in civilian dress were waiting. Andrus Hoggard must have had a lot of family and friends, I thought.

I was about to join the back of the queue when I saw a member of the Fertillan Guard striding towards me. I felt a sudden sense of anxiety, even though I hadn't done anything wrong, but as he got nearer, I caught a glimpse of Stephen's face between the peak of his hat and the top of his buttoned-up collar.

"Cassy," he said. "Glad you could make it."

I made an effort to smile, despite my nerves. "I was in Londos anyway so it wasn't a problem."

"Quite so."

Standing next to him, only a day after our sensuous kiss, was exciting, yet confusing. I still didn't know how I was going to ask him the questions I needed to ask him.

"Shall we go in?" he said.

Stephen led me to the front of the queue where, much to my relief, we bypassed a security team searching everyone as they passed through the entrance. The real reason why, it seemed, it was taking so long for everyone to file inside.

The main room of the chapel was long with rows of bench seating on either side of a central aisle that led to a small raised platform with a lectern. Behind the lectern was the machine where Hoggard's body lay hidden and, just in front of it, was a man in civilian clothes who was looking down the aisle directly at us.

"If you'll excuse me," said Stephen. "I have matters to attend to. I'll see you after the ceremony."

"Yes, see you then."

As Stephen walked down the aisle, I felt the warmth of his presence dissipate. It was like I had stepped into a cold room.

The man in civilian dress greeted Stephen and I saw the family resemblance immediately: it was Prince James. Both men had the trademark wide Regellan nose and blue eyes, but James had let his brown hair grow longer than Stephen's military style and he was a little taller. He was also dressed in notable royal finery. The colours were dark and sombre to mark the occasion, but they had a sense of opulence about them with the use of expensive iridescent fabric cut perfectly to hide his slightly over-developed belly. Even his shoes, I noted, were made of a polished material that could possibly have been real cattle leather. They had a substantial built up heel which suggested he wasn't actually any taller than Stephen, he just liked to appear that way.

Someone bumped into me from behind. It was an old woman, considerably shorter than me and twice as wide. "You can't stand there," she said.

I was blocking the way of people coming through the security check and so I stepped to the side. The wide woman hustled past and hunted for a seat in the quickly filling rows of the chapel. I realised if I didn't sit down soon, I might not get the opportunity to sit down at all, so I found a space in the middle of a row not far from the front, apologised to people as I squeezed past them, and sat down.

The room began to settle. Stephen and James sat down in the reserved seating on the front row next to a woman holding a baby, and the ceremony began.

A succession of family and friends stood at the lectern and shared their memories of the man they knew as 'Andi'. I heard how he was a clever man and a caring man. He was a son to be proud of, a brother to look up to, a husband to treasure and a father who was thrilled at the birth of his first son. A father who will now never see his little boy grow up. At the mention of the child, some of the people on the benches looked across at the woman with the baby who had to be Hoggard's widow. Every now and again the boy let out a little cry and she soothed him by bouncing him up and down on her lap.

Prince James was the last to speak. When he stood and walked to the front, a reverential quiet fell upon the chapel. Nervous coughs were silenced, the sniffs of people trying to hold back tears stopped and even the baby's cries ceased for a little while. It was an extraordinary display of how much power he commanded just by his royal presence.

Prince James told his assembled subjects how Hoggard had been a loyal and trusted colleague in the royal household, to the point where he had become a friend. James listed many of his achievements, recounted a funny story about Hoggard mixing up the sleeping arrangements of visiting dignitaries, and praised him to heights that no ordinary person could be capable of. James was an accomplished speaker and held such authority that it was difficult to know where the truth stopped and the lies began.

"It is a matter of personal regret," James continued, "that it was on a royal mission where Andi met such a senseless death. His loyalty and devotion to the very end is something all of us can be proud of. I hope his wife, Marée, can take some comfort at knowing that, to his last, he was serving Fertilla to the upmost of his ability and his sacrifice will not be forgotten."

James's voice cracked through the last few words as if he were overcome with emotion and, as he looked down at Hoggard's widow sitting in the front row, the glimmer of tears appeared in his eyes.

It was an accomplished performance. James had turned the raised platform into a stage and told a story that was totally believable to anyone who didn't know the truth.

After the speeches, the mourners were allowed a moment of quiet reflection. Then a young girl, who someone behind me muttered was Hoggard's niece, stepped up to the front and sang unaccompanied with a clear angelic voice. Her soaring soprano notes resonated around the chapel and masked the sound of people who couldn't hold back their tears any longer. In the background, the soft whirring of the machine turned Hoggard's body to ash. It was very moving.

At the end of the song, Prince Stephen, Prince James and Marée Hoggard with her baby all made their way down the aisle and out of the double doors. I stood up to follow them, but so did everyone else and it took me many minutes to exit the building.

Eventually, I was able to join the throng of people milling around outside. I saw Stephen was standing by the two parked vehicles and watching the crowd as Prince James got into the lead car. Meanwhile, Marée Hoggard was standing with her baby resting on her shoulder at the head of a makeshift queue of well-wishers taking turns to tell her how sorry they were about her husband. I decided Stephen could wait and I stood in line to offer my condolences.

Marée looked weary. She was marginally shorter than me, but the weight of her grief and being at the funeral seemed to have shrunk her further. Her eyes were small and red from where she had been crying and her face was pale. I imagined having to stand there with all those people telling her they were sorry was more of a burden than a comfort. She stared at me blankly. She had no idea who I was, and nor should she have. It was all washing over her.

I leant forward and cooed at her baby. "Isn't he adorable?" I said, mimicking what I had heard other women say. He was, actually, very cute, but as I stroked his soft pale cheek and he wriggled away from my finger, I was able to get my face close to Marée's ear and whisper, "I was there when your husband died. If you want to know his last words, find me in the chapel."

As I withdrew, she watched me with questioning eyes. I knew she had understood.

I sneaked back into the chapel through the double doors. It was empty and the lights were dimmed to near twilight. Even the machine was silent. I found a space on a bench at the back and waited.

Minutes later, Marée slipped inside, cradling her baby who looked like he was drifting off to sleep.

I stood as she looked around, but when she saw me, she didn't come any closer. She just let the door close behind her.

"Who are you?" she demanded in a loud, unrestrained voice.

I stepped towards her and kept my voice low. "My name is Sesaan Cassandra."

She seemed unimpressed. "Prince James said no one was with Andi when he died. He said no one was there to hear his last words."

"I'm afraid that's not true," I said.

I expected her to call me a liar. In her position, I wouldn't have believed a stranger over a prince who had just given an award-winning performance. But, instead, she sighed, like she had expected to hear it. "I see."

She came further into the chapel and sat on the bench opposite.

"I need to put Robbi down, he's getting so heavy now." The little boy squirmed in her arms as she placed him beside her on the hard seat. She cradled his head in her palm to make a little pillow and he made a tiny sighing noise as she did so, but he didn't wake.

"You were really with Andi when he died?" she asked.

I came to stand beside her. "Yes," I said.

"Was it really a street fight?"

It was the first indication that she doubted the story Prince James had told everyone. "I wasn't there when he was wounded. I only found him afterwards. I'm sorry I couldn't do anything to save him."

"But he said something?"

"He said, 'deliver the code'. He said it was important, that it was 'our salvation'. Do you know what that means?"

She smiled and dropped her head like she was disappointed, but also expecting it. "He didn't say anything about me and Robbi?"

I wish I could have made up a comforting lie to tell her, but if she knew anything about the code, I had to make her tell me. I hadn't any time to make up stories. "I'm sorry, he didn't."

"Well," she said. "Thank you for telling me."

She gathered her baby in her arms and stood up, but she couldn't get back out into the aisle because I was standing in the way. I didn't move. "You must know what he meant. You must know why he went to Serilla. If he told anyone, he would have told you."

"Prince James said he was on a royal mission."

"And you believe him?"

I swear I saw in her face that she didn't. I swear that, behind her blank tear-stained expression, there was something she wasn't telling me. "It doesn't matter now. Andi is dead. Robbi and me still have our lives and the prince has been very good to us."

"Don't you want to know the truth?" I said.

"The only truth anyone needs to know is my husband died on a mission for the royal family."

I saw her inner strength as she stood before me. She seemed to grow taller in defiance and I knew that, if she knew anything, she wasn't going to confess it to a stranger.

I had no choice but to step aside and let her leave.

Chapter Twenty

STEPHEN STOOD WITH his hands clasped behind his back, pacing back and forth in front of the only remaining military vehicle parked outside of the Celebration of Life Chapel.

He smiled as I approached. "Cassy! I was afraid you might have left."

"No, I got stuck in the crowd." It wasn't a bad excuse and he seemed to take it at face value.

"I thought I might offer you a lift back to your accommodation."

I hesitated. I had planned to ask him about the code, but after my lack of success with Hoggard's widow, I didn't know what to say to him. "It's okay, I can walk."

"Of course, you *can* walk," said Stephen. "But why walk, when you can ride?"

He stepped over to the rear door of the car and opened it to reveal the seat inside.

The driver jumped out of the front seat like it was on fire and rushed around to where we were standing. Stephen allowed the flustered man to take the door handle from him and the driver stood to attention while I got inside. He then opened the door on the other side to allow Stephen to get in.

All a bit ridiculous, really, as we were both adults perfectly capable of opening doors for ourselves, but he seemed very keen to do it for us.

As Stephen sat next to me and the door shut behind him, I became aware of how close he was to me in that small space. I caught a hint of his masculine scent and my body reacted, even though I didn't want it to.

"Where is it you're staying?" asked Stephen.

I told him Mandi's address, which he relayed to the driver and I felt the rumble of the electric motor beneath me as the car set off.

It was a slow process, as there were still people leaving the chapel grounds, but we made it out into the street. Not that we were able to pick up much speed, as people in Londos are not used to vehicles getting in the way of where they're walking. The driver kept having to slow while people noticed the car was heading for them and dashed out of the way.

"I'm glad you could come," said Stephen.

"I didn't realise he had a wife and baby," I said. "Why did he do it when he had a young family? Steal the thing he stole, I mean."

"Why do people do anything?" said Stephen.

That wasn't helpful. I needed to fish for information without sounding like I was fishing for information. It was like trying to traverse a wormhole without a QED. "What was it that he stole?"

"Something that annoyed my brother."

"Oh," I said.

"I couldn't tell you what it was, Cassy, even if I knew."

I needed to ask him what he thought about a new food technology with the potential to feed the Rim. Given the circumstances, it was an impossible question to ask. As I tried to think of a different way to approach the subject, he reached his hand across the car seat and clasped my fingers. His hand was warm where mine was cold. It was comforting and sensual – and I wanted to touch more of his body right there, even though there was a driver in the front seat and there were people in the streets who could see us through the windows.

"What are we doing?" I said.

"Driving back to your guest house," said Stephen.

"No, I meant…" I squeezed his hand. I looked at the driver up front, sitting within earshot, and I dared not say any more.

"I like you," said Stephen.

I was flattered, but I also felt out of place in the back seat of the car with him. "Our lives are so very different."

"In some ways," he said. "In other ways the same."

"Your brother's the King, you command a whole planet's worth of Fertillan Guard. I'm just a freelance spaceship captain."

"A prince's life can be lonely sometimes. Like it must be lonely being a freelance spaceship captain."

"I have Freddi," I said.

"A man twice your age – if not more."

"And friends all over the Rim. Like Nanci. We'll collect our ship soon, have a drink with her and listen to some of her crazy stories before we head off again."

"That's what I mean," said Stephen. "You're always on the move. How often do you see Nanci? Or any of your friends? How can you ever form a meaningful relationship?"

I pulled my hand back into my lap. "I have a good life."

"That's what they say about me."

"They're not wrong, are they?"

"I was born into a privileged position," he said. "People do what I say, even if they think it is stupid – even if they think it will get them killed, sometimes. I have every material thing I could want – tea and honey twenty-four hours a day if I like – but there's no excitement, there's no spark!"

"Is that what I am? A bit of excitement?"

"I don't know what you are, Cassy. Not yet. But I'd like to find out."

That was the bit that scared me. Out in space, I knew the order of things and where I stood in relation to them. Forming a relationship with a prince would be a journey into the unknown.

I sat up in my seat and looked around at the streets we were driving through. "I think we're nearly here," I said.

Stephen peered out of the window. "One more street, I think."

"You can't get the car down there," I said. "At least, you can't turn round and come out easily. Anyway, I'd rather not be seen by other people at the guest house."

By which I meant Mandi. She would want to ask questions and I definitely didn't want to answer them.

Stephen instructed the driver to park up on the adjoining street.

"I'll walk with you for the last bit," he said.

"I can find my own way," I said.

"I don't doubt it."

The driver got out the car and opened the door at Stephen's side so he got out first and I couldn't make a quick getaway.

When the driver let me out of the other side, I realised people in the street were staring. Stephen had pulled the peak of his hat down even further over his eyes and was looking at his boots. I don't think anyone had recognised him as they were more interested in the unusual sight of the car.

I felt their eyes watching me as I led Stephen into the street where Mandi's house was. When we were out of sight of them, Stephen reached out for my hand and I allowed his touch to warm my fingers as we walked together to Mandi's door.

I pressed my palm on the lockpad – Mandi programmed the pad with all her guests' prints while they were staying there – the locks disengaged and the door opened a crack.

"Thanks for the lift," I said.

"Are you not going to invite me in?" said Stephen.

"It's a bit…" It was hard to describe Mandi's place without being rude. "It's not exactly a palace."

"I'm not entirely spoilt, you know, Cassy. Being in the Fertillan Guard has taken me to many places more inhospitable than this."

I pushed the door open and allowed him to follow me inside. He closed the door behind us and I stood somewhat nervously with the prince in the tiny entranceway.

"Outside in the street, I couldn't do this," he said. He leant forward and kissed me. It was a brief kiss. Hardly had his lips touched mine than he had withdrawn them again, but it was enough to send a rush of hormones running round my body.

"You mean…" I stood on my tiptoes so my face was level with his. "You couldn't do this."

I returned the kiss, but went in stronger and harder. I pressed my mouth against his and put my hand onto the back of his neck to pull him closer.

The brim of his hat hit my forehead. He grabbed hold of it with one hand and dropped it on the floor while the other clasped my waist and pulled me in close. My breasts touched his chest and, even through the material of my shirt and his jacket, the fire inside of me burned fiercer; hungry for fuel. Snatching breaths where we could, our tongues entwined as we grasped each other with such long-hidden desire that we could barely stand, and stumbled until my back touched the cold wall behind me. I fumbled at the scratchy material of his jacket, feeling for a way past his stiff uniform, until I slipped my hand up inside from the gap at his waist, tore at his shirt until it came free from where it was tucked into his waistband and I felt his naked, sweaty back.

With one hand resting on the wall, he used his other to pop open a button of my shirt and slipped it inside to cup my breast. I couldn't help but sigh with pleasure. I was ready to rip off my clothes, rip off his clothes, get naked on the floor, on the stairs – wherever – and ride him until our bodies exploded like a supernova. But, as I briefly opened my eyes, I saw the redecorated image of my childhood home and was acutely aware of where we were.

Battling my primal instincts – still breathing heavily with excitement and with my blood rushing through my body – I placed my hand over his fingers and stopped him fondling my breast.

"Don't you want me to?" His breath was warm on my face as he spoke. "Is it too much?"

"No…" I breathed. "Yes… I mean, I want you to, but we can't… not here. Not with your driver outside."

I let go and his hand slipped from my breast, leaving a gap in my shirt for the air to rush in and chill my flesh. He stepped away and my fingers relinquished their hold on his back.

We stood before each other; red-faced, dishevelled and holding back our unfulfilled lust. He reached down for his hat, smoothed back his hair and pressed it onto his head. "Maybe my place," he said.

"Yes."

"Or your ship."

"Yes."

He tucked his shirt back into his trousers and pulled down his jacket.

I went to do up the button on my shirt, but it had pinged off somewhere and so I clasped the two sides together to restore some kind of modesty.

"I'll see you again, then," he said, opening the door.

"Yes."

He looked at me like he wanted to say something else, but whatever it was he decided against it. He turned away and stepped out into the street.

I closed the door behind him, leant back on its cool, hard surface and breathed deeply.

A noise upstairs startled me. I looked up and saw Freddi standing on the top step, smiling and resting on the bannister with his arms folded. "I had a brother," he said. "But I never kissed him like that!"

Embarrassed, I pulled the two sides of my buttonless blouse closer together. "Half-brother," I corrected him. "And he's not, anyway, he told me."

"And you believe a member of the royal family with all their history of interbreeding?"

I trumped up the stairs until I was face to face with him. "Yes," I said. "I believe him."

Freddi reached into his pocket and pulled out a clean, white handkerchief. "I still think we should make sure," he said. He reached out for me with his handkerchief and, instinctively, I shied away from him. "No, don't move."

He was reaching for something on my shoulder and, because I have come to trust Freddi with my life, I held still while he touched me.

He pulled the handkerchief back and opened up the material to reveal a human hair lying on its white surface. The hair was short and brown, not long and dark like mine.

"I still think we should run a test to make sure," he said. "Don't you?"

<h1 style="text-align:center">Chapter Twenty One</h1>

I DIDN'T EXPECT EVER to hear from Marée Hoggard again, but the morning after the funeral, I found a message from her on my P-tab. She apologised for the way she had acted in the chapel, but she said it had been a very difficult day and she had been upset. She wanted to meet on neutral territory that evening where we could talk without the risk of other people overhearing.

I hid the memory ball safely in the pocket of my other trousers hung up in the wardrobe and strapped my EE handgun to my thigh. I preferred not to carry a gun on a planet like Fertilla as it could attract the wrong kind of attention, but there was something about the message that made me want to have it at my side. I had a licence for a personal EEW and, as long as I kept it peace bonded with the strap around the hilt so a chancer couldn't grab it, I could avoid getting arrested.

Freddi had gone into the centre of Londos to find what he called "a decent meal and a beer", so I left a note to say I might be late back and headed out to an industrial area which I knew, at that time of day, would be virtually empty. Around me, the lights of Londos dimmed and ushered in the evening. I let my P-tab guide me through the twists and turns through the middle of the industrial area and right out to the far edge where there were no lights at the windows and it had been at least ten minutes since I had seen a shift worker dashing into one of the buildings.

I looked down at my P-tab – the light from its screen brighter than the evening gloom around me – and checked the address. It should have been one of the doorways set back from the big block in front of me, that rose up to almost touch the Londos ceiling. I walked steadily forward and looked at the first doorway, but there was no handle or buzzer on the outside and was probably some sort of fire escape or emergency exit. I kept walking.

Two figures emerged from the shadows of the second door-way. They were dressed head to toe in dark clothing with scarves wrapped around their faces so only their eyes stared out. I stopped dead. This was no rendezvous, this was an ambush.

The click of an opening door behind me made me shudder. I turned to see two more masked figures emerge from what, moments before, had been an empty doorway. I reached for my holster and flicked off the peace-bonding strap.

"Gun!" shouted one of them behind me.

I grabbed the hilt and pulled my weapon ready to fire, but something sharp hit my back.

Muscles clenched between my ribs as the electric current of a taser fired into my flesh.

My whole body spasmed. I tried to lift my gun. I tried to pull the trigger, but my arm was useless: it wouldn't obey me.

My frozen legs were unable to hold my weight and I collapsed to my knees. I didn't feel my gun slip from my powerless fingers, but I heard it clatter to the ground and knew I was disarmed. The relentless *click, click, click* of the taser's current cramping every muscle in my body sent me crashing forward. Without the use of my hands to stop myself, my face struck the hard surface of the street.

I quivered in the grip of the taser until the clicking stopped and I was in the aftershock of cramp.

Someone pulled my hands behind my back and wrapped something tight around my numb wrists. Something was put over my head – a bag of thick cloth – and a cord tied tight around my neck. My senses, already dulled by the effect of the taser, became deadened to the sights and sounds around me.

I struggled to get free, but I was like a jellyfish caught in a net and the four of them easily over-powered me.

Two of them grabbed hold of an arm each and pulled me to my feet by my armpits. I cried out and the sound of my own voice was muffled by the bag. They dragged me to what had to be one of the doorways, where my feet struck a step and I was forced inside the building.

"Where are you taking me?"

No one answered.

"What do you want?"

My feet found the floor and took some of my weight, but I was immediately pulled forward again and was half dragged, as I half stumbled, to wherever it was we were going.

Not far, I think. Down a corridor and into a room.

The men carrying me – I'm fairly sure they were men – dumped me down onto a hard chair and put my bound hands behind its upright back. With sensation returning to my body, I stood up again; intending to run at them and hurt them and somehow escape, but strong hands pushed me back. Some sort of rope was wound around my body and pulled tight before being knotted behind me.

I kicked out my feet, but they were grabbed and bound to the legs of the chair. I'm fairly sure I managed to kick one of them in the face, though.

I sat with my body and ankles secured to the chair with my hands tied behind it; breathing deeply. My breaths were magnified inside the confines of the bag and made it harder to hear what was happening. I forced myself to be calm, to ease my breathing, so I could hear and so I could think.

The four of them were talking in hushed tones, so I couldn't hear what they were saying. But there was definitely just the four of them, and at least one of them was a woman. I was still very out-numbered, even if I hadn't been incapacitated.

"What the vac is going on?" I shouted within my bag and struggled against my bonds.

Footsteps came towards me. I flinched away from them and my back pressed against the upright of the chair.

"What do you know about the code?" said a male voice.

I knew then what I had suspected ever since the first masked figure emerged from the shadows of the doorway. Marée hadn't asked me there to meet her. I was lured there.

"Who wants to know?" I demanded.

"I do," said the voice.

"Why should I tell you?"

"Because you want to live."

My muscles clenched, and this time not from the taser.

They had me helpless and they could kill me as easily as whoever it was had killed Hoggard. I had to be smart if I was going to get through this.

I heard a second male voice, probably about the same distance away as the first man, but speaking low. They were consulting with each other, I presumed.

It was the first male voice that spoke again to me. "Marée said you were with Andi Hoggard when he died."

"Are you friends of hers?"

"That doesn't matter. What matters is that you answer my question."

"Yeah, I was with him," I admitted. It wasn't a secret. Trevel of the Fertillan Guard had found me there after all.

"Did you kill him?" said the voice.

"No! Why would I tell his widow I was there if I was the one who had killed him?"

"Because of the code."

The second voice spoke again. Loud enough, this time, for me to catch part of the sentence. Although 'Marée' and 'last words' were all I could hear. The man was still breathing heavily from having dragged me inside. If it did come down to a fight, I thought, at least I was fitter than him.

"What did he say to you before he died?" said the first voice.

"He asked me to deliver the code. He said it was our salvation. But it didn't mean anything to me. I told Marée all this freely, without having to be dragged off the street."

"How can we believe you?"

"Because… because it's true!"

"Why would he say that to you of all people?"

"I don't know," I said. "Because I was the only one there, I suppose."

The second voice spoke again. His breath was still laboured and it had been many minutes since I was attacked – far longer than it should have taken for even an unfit man to recover. Then I realised he wasn't breathing heavily, he was wheezing. He wasn't just unfit, he had some sort of respiratory condition. I listened harder and recognised the tones of a voice I had heard before.

"Is that Brimble?" I said.

The kerfuffle of the other two people in the room, hitherto silent, told me I had hit a nerve.

"What is a Brimble?" said the first voice. But even as he denied knowledge of the name, the way he said it told me he was lying.

"It *is* Brimble, isn't it? Does Prince Stephen know you are here? Does Prince Stephen know you're doing this?"

Footsteps belonging to the two men who had spoken to me backed away. A discussion, too muffled to make out clearly, broke out at what sounded like the back of the room. I heard only the occasional word: one of which was definitely 'idiot'.

Their panicked voices died down and one clear and wheezy voice shouted above them. "Everybody out!"

I listened, but nothing happened.

"Out! Out! All of you!" said the voice I was sure belonged to Brimble.

There was movement, a door opening and closing. Then one set of footsteps approached me. I heard his wheezy breath; he was very close.

Something cold and sharp touched my neck. A knife.

"No! Please!" I turned my head away from him, but my torso was still tied to the chair and I couldn't get away.

"Hold still, Cassy. I don't want to cut you."

He slipped the blade of the knife between my neck and the cord of the bag and I stopped wriggling as he cut through.

The cord was severed. The bag was loose. He pulled it off of my head.

I sucked in the dry air outside of the dampness of the bag which had been filled with the moisture of my own breath, as my eyes adjusted to the light of the room I was sitting in.

It was a large space that maybe had been some kind of factory at one time, but looked abandoned. There were a few bits of furniture left behind, some lights shining down from overhead and one man standing in front of me dressed head to toe in dark clothing.

"Hello, Cassy," said Brimble.

CHAPTER TWENTY TWO

BRIMBLE FOUND A chair in the abandoned factory where I was being held and set it in front of me. He sat down, took off the flat cap he was wearing and folded it in his hands.

He looked different than he did when I had seen him in Londos House. His clothes were cheap, a little tatty, and the impassive face that I was used to had been replaced with an anxious expression.

I was still tied to the chair. I wriggled my wrists and loosened them a little, but they were bound with some kind of strong adhesive tape and it would be a long while before I could free them. Rope around my chest kept my body tight against the chair back and my ankles were still tied to the chair legs. I would need to talk my way out of this one.

"What the vac are you doing?" I glared at him. Blood from where I had bashed my nose on the ground outside ran down onto my upper lip. I licked it away and swallowed its unpleasant saltiness.

"We need to know about the code, Cassy," wheezed Brimble.

"And you couldn't just ask me?"

"We didn't know if we could trust you."

"So you kidnapped me?"

"You are close to Prince Stephen. We couldn't risk it."

I sighed. That relationship was definitely more trouble than it was worth. "This has nothing to do with him, then?"

"This has nothing to do with him," confirmed Brimble.

"Can you untie me?"

"I could, but my friends wouldn't like it."

"Who are your friends?"

"Friends," he said.

"Look, Brimble–" I began. "Do you have a first name?"

"Davvid."

"Look, Davvid, if you want me to be honest with you, then you have to be honest with me. At the very end, Hoggard trusted me, so I'm going to ask you to trust me too. Tell me what the vac your little group is up to and I will tell you what I know."

"You first," he said.

"How do I know you won't just kill me afterwards?"

"Trust runs both ways."

I sighed. I was the one tied up and I knew I had little to bargain with. So I told him how Hoggard had disguised himself as a monk to buy passage on board my ship. I told him how he had created a diversion when we landed at Serilla and how the Fertillan Guard had come looking for him. I told him how I was called to his side while he lay dying and how he told me to deliver the code.

"Why you?" said Brimble.

"I think he knew he was at risk," I said. "So he hid the code on my ship, and I imagine he planned to come back for it.

However, the Fertillan Guard came looking for him soon after he left the ship and then someone stuck a knife in his back within hours of him arriving at Serilla."

Brimble stood from his chair. "You have the code?"

"Yes. That's why I wanted to know what he meant by his last words."

"Where is it?" Brimble demanded.

"I'm not going to tell you until you tell me why it's so important to you."

"I can't."

"If you think I'm going to tell Prince Stephen, then you don't have to worry. I haven't told him any of this."

"But you and His Majesty…?"

"I only kissed him," I said. "I didn't swear allegiance to him. Unlike you."

Brimble walked around his chair. Twice. Then sat down again.

He drew in a wheezy breath. "Andi Hoggard was my friend," he said. "We both worked in the Regellan royal household. In fact, I trained him when he first joined, before he went to work for Prince James. There was a secret some of us knew about. We called it, 'the code'. It was… important. Prince James had ordered it destroyed because he knew its existence threatened the rule of the Regellans. Their wealth, and their power, comes from the farming economy on Fertilla. The only place you can grow food is inside an agro-dome. The only way you can set up an agro-dome is with the permission of the royal household. The only way a farmer can sell what he grows is by paying taxes to the Regellan family. Without that stranglehold on food production on Fertilla, the King and the princes would see their power wither to nothing. They know that."

"That's what Hoggard stole?" I said. "A code that would make agro-domes and Fertilla's food economy obsolete."

"Yes," said Brimble. "All the copies of it were destroyed long ago, but we secretly kept one. Andi was going to meet a contact on Serilla and take it to where the knowledge could be used to benefit everyone. I said he shouldn't go, not with a young son waiting for him at home. I said I would do it. But he argued I was too old, that my physical condition meant I couldn't run if I had to, let alone fight. We argued a lot about it. In the end, he left without telling me. I suspect Prince James had found out and Andi had to leave in a hurry, but I don't know for sure."

"Now you want to know what happened to the code," I suggested.

"When Andi died, we believed he had failed and the code was lost or stolen. Then we found out he had said something to you before he died and... well, you know the rest."

"I can take it to your contact on Serilla."

"You can?" His optimism was fleeting. "Except Serilla isn't safe after what happened to Andi. Our contact could be compromised or dead."

"Then to wherever it needs to go. I have a spaceship. Repairs are complete. We can leave tomorrow – tonight, if we have to."

"Why would you do that?" said Brimble.

"Because I care about the future of people living on the Rim."

"What about Prince Stephen?"

"He's a very sexy man," I admitted. "But I wouldn't sell out millions of people to spend the rest of my life sitting around a palace drinking tea and honey."

Brimble took in a wheezy breath.

He looked down at where he was clasping his cap. He turned it over in his hands. "I'll have to consult with the others."

Brimble stood up and walked out of the room.

I strained against my bonds. One foot was almost free, but every time I twisted my hands, the restraints around my wrists seemed to dig in tighter.

It was only moments before Brimble came back in. I couldn't tell by his face if he was going to free me or if he was going to kill me. He stopped a metre away, just behind the chair where he had been sitting.

"We agree," he said. "But I need to come with you."

Relief spread through my body and my muscles relaxed like the opposite of being hit by the electric current of a taser.

"You have a shuttle at Angellis Port to take you to your ship?"

"Yes," I said.

"I'll meet you there first thing in the morning. It's an open and busy space, and I have a friend who works there, so I will know if you double-cross me."

"I won't."

"And you won't say anything to Prince Stephen?"

"I've kept it secret from him until now."

Brimble nodded. He reached down beside my chair and picked up the black bag where he had dropped it. "I'm sorry, but it's important you don't see the others. Just in case."

He put the bag back over my head and darkness returned. I shuddered as I heard more approaching footsteps which were muffled by the material around my ears. But all they did was untie my ankles, take off the rope from around my chest, and lift me to my feet. The same two people who had dragged me in there, allowed me to walk as they each took an arm and guided me out into street.

"Get on your knees!" ordered the voice belonging to the first man who had questioned me.

Suddenly terrified that they were going to execute me after all, I stumbled backwards and struck a wall I couldn't see. "Why?"

"Just do it." A foot kicked at the back of my knees and I went down hard on my knee caps. Someone grabbed my wrists at the back of me and I felt a sharp knife cut through my bonds. My hands were free.

"Go!" said the voice and I heard them run off.

I pulled the bag off of my head and turned to see four figures running down the street. Three of them turned a corner at the end, while a slower forth one struggled to keep up with them. Brimble, I assumed.

I stood and my foot kicked something on the ground beside me. It was my EE handgun. I picked it up, but I didn't put it in my holster. I carried it as I ran all the way back to Mandi's house.

CHAPTER TWENTY THREE

I THREW OPEN THE door to Freddi's room where he was sleeping. He hardly had time to stir before I grabbed his clothes off the chair and flung them at him. He was just lifting his head off the pillow and got a shirt right in the face.

"Get dressed. We're leaving."

I turned on the light.

He pulled the shirt from his face and squinted into the brightness. "What, now?"

"Yes now."

He sat up fully in bed, but kept the covers over his bottom half.

"What happened to your face?" he asked.

I touched my upper lip and felt the blood that had dried there. "Drakh!" I had forgotten about that.

I pulled open the wardrobe door assuming that, like mine, it had a mirror on the inside. I peered into the small square reflective surface and winced at my bloodied nose which was starting to go an ugly bruised brown.

I closed the wardrobe door and turned to see Freddi standing there. He was looking straight at me with concerned eyes. "I asked what happened."

"I fell," I said, covering my lie in a half-truth. I turned away but he grasped my elbow and pulled me back.

He lifted my arm so it was between us. I had ripped the bits of tape from my wrists as I ran back, but I couldn't erase the red marks where I had been tied up. Those, too, had started to bruise. "What happened to you, Cassy?"

I yanked my elbow free. "I don't want to talk about it. Get packed and send a message to Nanci to say we'll be coming for our ship. I'll settle up with Mandi and we'll be out of here in half an hour."

"Yes, Captain," said Freddi.

I walked out to hide my embarrassment and headed to my room to start packing.

I PACED UP and down the entrance to the shuttle, waiting for Brimble. Freddi was inside at the controls, making sure everything was ready for our departure.

Brimble was right about Angellis Port being a busy place, even at that time in the morning. Not that the time meant anything to people arriving from outside of the Fertillan system. Most humans stick to twenty-four hours in a day, but out in the Rim, spacefarers don't have to sync those twenty-four hours with Fertilla or any planet. So, early in the morning for us, might not be early in the morning for them.

Also, Brimble's idea of 'first thing' could mean anything. I hoped it meant very vacking soon, as I wanted to get off Fertilla as soon as possible. I may have been honest when I said I wouldn't double-cross him, but I had no reason to trust that he had similar honourable intentions. The only thing that gave me faith was the knowledge of what was contained in the code and how we both seemed to want it to end up in the right hands.

Freddi emerged from the interior of the shuttle. "Ready when you are," he said.

"Good," I said. I kept pacing.

"Who's this passenger?" he asked.

"Davvid Brimble."

"And who's he?"

"He works – or worked, probably now – for Prince Stephen."

"He should be able to pay us a decent fee, then."

I stopped pacing. "I suspect not."

"What do you mean, 'suspect'?" said Freddi. "You do remember that you offered me a pay rise, don't you?"

"There he is!" I pointed out onto the concourse where a thin man was struggling to pull a wheeled cart loaded with three bags past some of the other crews going back and forth with supplies.

"Hmm," said Freddi. "Not what I was expecting."

"What were you expecting?"

"Someone with less luggage."

Brimble wheezed his way through and stopped at the bottom

of the ramp, gasping for air. He put his hand out on the side of the hull and looked up at us; red faced.

"I don't suppose," he gasped, "someone could help me with my bags?"

"I can do that," said Freddi. He hobbled down the ramp with that swinging walk he has and made the three journeys necessary to bring Brimble's luggage on board. By which time, Brimble had recovered enough to make his way up the ramp.

When he had both feet firmly over the threshold, Freddi hit the control to close the bay door and I pulled my EE weapon from its holster and pointed it at Brimble.

Brimble's hands shot up in defence, he took a step backwards and almost tripped over one of his own bags.

Freddi stared at me in disbelief. "What the vac, Cassy?"

"Search him," I said.

"I thought you said you know this person," said Freddi.

"Don't argue – search him!"

Freddi raised his eyebrows at me, but still stepped towards Brimble. "Whatever you say, Captain."

Brimble's hands remained in the air as he trembled and stared at my EEW. He shuddered at the touch of Freddi patting his pockets.

"Search him properly, Freddi. Make sure he hasn't any weapons."

Freddi ran his hands down Brimble's trembling legs and arms and then across the main trunk of his body. "He's clean," he concluded as he stepped back.

I didn't lower my weapon for a second. "Now search his bags."

Freddi frowned at me, but did as I asked by squatting down in front of the first bag and unzipping the top. Inside was a selection of neatly packed clothes which Freddi began shifting through.

"No, a proper search!" I said. I walked over and kicked the bag out of Freddi's hands so everything flew out across the shuttle floor. They were almost all items of clothing, although there was also a hairbrush and what appeared to be a bag of toiletries. Freddi searched through it all, and checked the lining of the bag for any hidden surprises. He then gave me a disapproving look as he opened the other two bags and tipped out their contents.

"He hasn't got any weapons, Cassy," said Freddi when he completed his search.

"Good." I lowered my EEW and replaced it in my holster.

Brimble let out an audible sigh and lowered his arms.

"Let's get going," I said, and headed to the cockpit.

I climbed into the co-pilot's seat and, moments later, Freddi arrived to take the helm.

He swivelled his chair round to face me. I could see he was angry, but he kept his voice low to stop Brimble from overhearing. "What the vac was that, Cassy?"

"Being careful," I said.

"That's not being careful," said Freddi. "That's being paranoid."

"He's clean, what does it matter?"

"It matters because we're taking him into space with us and I need to sleep at night. You say you're bringing a passenger on board – that's fine. You say you know him and he's getting it cheap – as long as I get paid, that's your business. But when you're so scared, you have me search him like that – then I get worried, Cassy. If something goes wrong out in space, it's my neck as well as yours. You need to tell me what the vac is going on."

"When we're on the ship," I said.

"You tell me everything."

"I will, I promise."

Freddi swivelled back to face the controls and requested clearance to leave Fertilla.

We said nothing else, other than the perfunctory communications between pilot and co-pilot, all the way to Nanci's station.

Chapter Twenty Four

I T WAS GOOD to be back on the ship. My ship. My territory. My
rules.

We had to forgo our usual socialising with Nanci on the station. I missed her laugh, getting beaten at cards by her, and listening
to the new stories she had gathered since our last repair. But I wasn't
in the mood for it. We also had Brimble with us and he didn't look
like he had ever laughed in his life; especially at the sort of bawdy
stories Nanci liked to tell.

So I paid the hefty bill, gave Nanci a big hug and climbed
back aboard the metal enclosure I called home. All around me I
felt the reassuring rumble of the engines as Freddi took us out into
deep space ready to fire up the repaired QED and wormhole away.
It gave me a few moments to sit in my room: my newly restored,
slash-free room.

I tilted my head to the ceiling where Ship's speakers were.
"How are you feeling, Ship?" I asked.

"I do not have feelings, you know that, Cassy," she said.

I smiled at her reassuring voice. "Of course you don't, Ship. Did Nanci look after you?"

"My QED is repaired and I have plenty of fuel."

"That's good."

"She upgraded my security protocol so I can withstand future attacks. She also found a tracker on board which must have been placed there by the Fertillan Guard. I am sorry, Cassy, that I did not know it was there."

"The Fertillan Guard are cunning bastards. It wasn't your fault, Ship."

"I can report that it has been removed and destroyed."

"Very good," I said. "I missed you ever so much, Ship. You mean a lot to me, do you know that?"

"That's very human of you," she said.

I smiled. She was back to the old Ship. She didn't profess to love me or pretend to have any feelings of any kind.

I, on the other hand, was sitting on the floor full of trepidation.

In front of me was the box of my mother's things that the clothing factory manager had given me. I had barely thought about it from the moment I had stashed it under the bed in Mandi's house, but now I was alone in my room, I felt it was time to open up that part of my mother's past.

I ran my nail along the side to break the seal. I took a deep breath and lifted off the lid.

Underneath was a layer of tissue. I peeled it away gently to reveal a square of folded paper sitting atop a cushion of iridescent fabric, which was also folded neatly.

I took the paper from the box.

I held it for a moment; wondering what might be inside. A note, perhaps, written by my mother to whoever should find the box after her death. Gingerly, I unfolded it.

It was not a note. But a series of sketches of a man wearing a suit. There were separate drawings of the jacket and trousers with measurements scribbled next to them. It was a seamstress's pattern. In the top right-hand corner there was a name written in block capitals: '*JOHN*'. King John?

I traced my hand across its surface and tried to reach my mother through her writing. In my mind, I saw the image of her from the photograph Stephen had shown me and remembered how she had stared at the camera with sad eyes.

I put the pattern on the floor and picked up the material. It unfolded itself into the shape of a jacket which had been tacked together with large, neat stitches in a white thread to contrast against the black of the material. Inside was a lining of dark rich blue that shimmered under the lights of my room.

I laid the jacket on my bed and reached into the box for the next piece of folded material. It was a pair of trousers in the same fabric. Unlike the jacket, the trousers seemed to have been finished, all but the seams at the bottom of each leg which had been tacked up with temporary stitches. I put them aside and looked into the bottom of the box.

All that was left was a reel of thread with a needle sticking out of it, a box of pins and a few scraps of different coloured material sewn into a fan with a handwritten label which said 'bedspread swatches'.

It was her work box. I felt disappointed.

I don't know what else I had expected to find from the place where she used to work.

I wanted a personal letter written to me. I wanted her to tell me who was my real father. I wanted her to explain why she let me stay over at my school friend's place the night our house caught fire. I wanted her to apologise for not keeping me there and allowing me to save her when the flames ripped through her bedroom.

Tears were in my eyes. Tears that I hadn't cried since I was an orphaned child and dreamt of what might have been as I lay in my tiny bed trying not to let on to the other girls.

My expectations had been foolish. The box contained the last item of clothing she had been making for King John. A suit she never completed because of that evil, wicked fire which had caused so much disruption.

The click of the communicator startled me. Freddi's voice came over the speaker. "Hi, Cassy, we're approaching the point where we're going to go to full stop, if you want to come up here."

I sniffed to clear my airway from the effects of my tears. "I'll be there in a minute."

"Brimble has the details of where he wants to go, but he won't give them to me – he says he'll only give them to you – so I haven't been able to calculate what we're going to need for the q-burst."

"Tell him he can trust you," I said.

"I did that. He doesn't believe me."

"I'll be there in a minute anyway."

"Okay," said Freddi and the communications cut out.

I folded up the unfinished suit and the pattern and put them back in the box. I replaced the lid and pushed it into the corner of my room out of the way.

I TOLD FREDDI what Brimble had told me in the abandoned factory. Freddi had forgiven me, I think, for not telling him the whole truth the night that I got him out of bed to leave Fertilla. He was the one, after all, who had persuaded me that the knowledge in the code was worth saving. If anyone was going to agree to a mission to deliver the code to where it needed to be, it was Freddi. Nevertheless, it had left our relationship a little strained.

Nanci's team had done a good job with the control room. All the inspection plates had been returned to their rightful positions and all the pirate brain had been cleaned off. It looked like nothing untoward had ever happened.

Freddi was at his usual console. Brimble was sitting at one of the positions we tended not to use when there were only the two of us. Not that he was paying any attention to the flight telemetry on the screen. He was facing the other way, towards the entrance, and saw me as soon as I came in.

"Cassy," said Brimble, standing up like a prince had just walked into the room.

Freddi turned his head with less reverence. "I've been trying to tell him we can't go to wherever it is we're going unless he tells me where it is."

Ship interrupted. "We are approaching the set deep space position. Readying for full stop."

The vibrations of the engines changed as they reversed thrust to slow us down.

I looked at Brimble. "So," I said. "Where is it that we are to deliver the code?"

He sat down. "There's a science research station in the Octavia system," he said. "Do you know it?"

I looked at Freddi. He shrugged.

"I don't think so," I said.

"It's a bit out of the way," said Brimble. "My understanding is, that was deliberate. The sun only has gas giants and a couple of scorching rocky worlds on inner orbit. There might be one or two small moons, I'm not sure. I'm led to believe there is a small population on a handful of orbiting space stations and converted ships. A perfect place for scientists to hide out without people bothering them."

He paused and took in a few wheezy breaths.

The engine vibrations stopped.

Brimble looked around; startled. "What's that?"

Ship replied. "We have reached full stop."

I walked over to my station and pulled up details on the Octavia system. It appeared to be an insignificant little outpost. I certainly had never been there, let alone heard of it.

At his console, I saw Freddi was looking at the same details. "These people are going to have the ability to harness the food technology in the code?" He sounded doubtful.

"Don't let their obscurity fool you," said Brimble. "Their contacts range wide across the Rim and they can attract talent which would rather not work for ruling families like the Regellans. A woman called Doctor Keya Sharma is the head of the research. I'm told if anyone can turn the code into reality, then it is her."

Freddi blew a whistle through his teeth as figures came up on the screen in front of him. "We're going to burn a lot of qubition to wormhole out there. Are you sure this Sharma woman is worth it?"

"Andi Hoggard died trying to get the code to her," said Brimble.

Freddi turned to me. "Cassy?"

"We've come this far," I said.

Freddi nodded. "I'll make the final calculations."

Numbers filled the screen in front of me. I looked across at Brimble who appeared small and fragile in the crew seat. "You might want to go to your room and lie down for when the QED kicks in and we fire the q-burst," I said.

"Does it hurt?" he said. "Going through a wormhole?"

"Oh yes," I said.

"Then I shall take your advice." Brimble stood and nodded to us both, like he had just served us tea, and walked out of the control room.

"Searching for potential wormholes," said Freddi. His fingers darted across his screen for several minutes before he found something. "Yeah, that should do it."

My screen showed the animated pattern of a wormhole opening near our position and emerging close to the Octavia system. More numbers – larger numbers than I was used to seeing – indicated the exact amount of qubition we needed to make the journey.

"Ready?" said Freddi.

"Oh yes," I said.

Freddi executed the commands and a q-burst engulfed our ship as if it had exploded us into little pieces while we simultaneously stayed intact. The qubition tore at the fabric of spacetime and thrust us into the passage of nothingness that was the wormhole; distorting me and everything around me in the agonising, glorious, supernatural pain of interstellar travel.

Chapter Twenty Five

The wormhole threw us out at a safe distance from the Octavia system and the pain of bending spacetime was over. I checked with Brimble over the communicator and he seemed shaken, but was alive and conscious which was enough to tell me he would be fine. The regular engines cut in and the whole ship was filled with their gentle rumble as we made our way through normal space.

I brought up a live image of the Octavia Research Station and zoomed in to see the detail. It was a long, spinal stem of a station with a large bulbous head at one end and lots of other thin, curved modules projecting out from the centre, all covered in solar panels. It spun on its axis to create gravity and the panels glinted in the light of the red giant sun behind.

Freddi also consulted his screen. "There's a lot of communication chatter coming from the station," he said. "Seems like a lively place."

"Let's hope that's a good thing," I said.

"I'll put in a request to dock and set a course. Do you want to compose a suitable message for the woman we're supposed to be meeting?"

"Doctor Keya Sharma," I said. It was very different to a Fertillan name and I had made a special effort to remember.

"It'll be some hours before we arrive," said Freddi. "I suggest you try to get some rest while you have the chance."

I suddenly realised how tired I was. I hadn't slept since the night before I was ambushed by Brimble and his friends, and my body was running on adrenaline. "You get some rest too, Freddi."

"I'm going to stay here for a bit, check out the neighbourhood; make sure we're not flying into any trouble. Then I'll take a nap."

I looked to the ceiling. "Make sure he does, Ship."

"I cannot make him do anything, Cassy. I can only remind him."

"Then make sure you do. And wake me if there's any trouble."

"Of course, Cassy," said Ship.

I sloped off to my room where I thought I might look up some more information about the Octavia Research Station. But as soon as I sat on my bed, I wanted to lie on it. As soon as I lay on it, I wanted to lie *in* it. I wriggled out of my clothes, climbed under the covers and slept.

Freddi woke me as we were coming in to dock. I quickly washed, winced at the sight of my ugly cut and bruised nose in the mirror and went up to the control room to help bring the ship in.

We docked without incident and, collecting Brimble on the way, went down to the bay where the doors opened onto a docking area so different from the ports at Serilla and Angellis that there was no comparison. There were no other ships, no people, just a high-ceilinged enclosure of functional grey metal, big enough for one light freighter and lit from above by harsh lighting.

I took the first step down the ramp and heard my footstep echo in the cavernous space. The men followed me and we descended onto the level floor of the space station. "Hello?" I called out.

A panel opened in the wall ahead of us and three women stepped out. They all wore the same white clothes, some sort of scientists' uniform I imagined, with a dark green logo in the shape of Octavia Research Station and the initials ORS printed on their right shoulders. I stopped. Freddi and Brimble stopped behind me, and we allowed the women to approach.

The one who seemed to be in charge had long black hair, darker than mine, which she had fashioned into a plait and wore draped across one shoulder and down to her chest. She wore make-up, which was something I rarely saw on the parts of the Rim I tended to visit, and it made the white of her teeth stand out against the red of her painted lips. She was immaculate, stunningly attractive and still only my age; maybe a little younger.

"Doctor Keya Sharma?" I asked.

She looked down at me and her eyes fixed at the EE handgun strapped to my thigh. "We do not allow weapons on Octavia," she said.

I had strapped it on out of habit and because it made me feel more secure after what had happened on my last night on Fertilla. My hand reached for it.

"No!" she said.

I froze.

"We'll take that for you."

One of the two women flanking either side of her stepped forward and I allowed her to reach for the gun in my holster. She pulled it out and held onto the barrel by her fingertips like it was some contaminated object.

"It will be returned to you on your departure," said the woman I assumed to be Keya Sharma. "Now, I believe you have brought something for us?"

"I have," I said. "It's in my pocket." Slowly, so as not to alarm them, I reached into my trouser pocket and pulled out the memory ball.

Her eyes widened as I held it out to her. "Amazing how something so small can contain something so valuable." She plucked it from my palm and held it up between her thumb and forefinger. It glinted in the harsh lighting; looking as shiny and new as it had on the day Nanci had given it to me. "I assume it contains what you claim it contains?"

Brimble stepped forward, bowed his head in respect and answered for me. "I know where the research came from. It is genuine."

"I see," said Keya. "You are Andrus Hoggard?"

"Unfortunately not," said Brimble. "He… couldn't make it."

I shivered involuntarily. It was cold standing in the docking area and I felt a little naked without the safety blanket of my gun.

"Let's go inside to talk," said Keya.

She led us towards the sliding door where she had entered, with her two colleagues in white following behind us. I expected to step into some sort of corridor or passage, but it was only a small, enclosed room. There was only one door – the one we were expected to enter – and room for about five people. Seeing as there were six of us, I hesitated.

"I thought this door would go somewhere," I said.

"It does," said Keya. "It goes up."

She must have seen my puzzled expression. "It's an elevator," she said. "Have you not been in one before?"

I relaxed as I realised how stupid I had been. "Not for a long time." I stepped in and held onto the rail which ran at waist height around the walls. Freddi, Brimble and the two women joined us and I pulled in my arms to minimise the space I was taking up as the door slid shut.

Keya spoke out above our heads. "Elevator," she said. "Authorisation Sharma to proceed to Level One with one EEW present."

I expected to feel the effect of the elevator moving, but all that happened was the strip of light which ran round the top of the walls turned from white to red and bathed us in a dusky glow.

An artificial voice spoke from above: "Bladed weapon detected."

The three women in white gazed suspiciously at us.

"Don't look at me!" said Brimble.

"You already have my weapon," I said.

We all stared at Freddi.

He held up his hands. "Sorry," he said. "I forgot I had it on me." Which was probably a lie.

He opened up the flap of his jacket, but before he could reach inside, the third woman (the one who hadn't disarmed me) reached forward and pulled out a fifteen-centimetre knife so sharp that it reflected back a beam of red light.

Keya gave him a displeased look. "Elevator," she said again. "Authorisation Sharma to proceed to Level One with one EEW and one bladed weapon present."

The strip of red light returned to white. The elevator jolted and motors whirred as we ascended further into the research station.

Within moments, the motors slowed and the elevator seemed to bounce a little as it came to a stop.

The door slid open and the two women, then Brimble and Freddi and finally myself and Keya stepped out with lighter, slightly bouncy steps. The gravity in this part of the station was less than I was used to and I put out a hand to touch the solid wall as my sense of balance adjusted.

We were standing in a corridor that seemed to curve up until it disappeared into nowhere. It took a moment for me work out that it had to be a passageway which ran around the central spinal column of the station. Doors were spaced at equal distances from each other down one side.

Keya dismissed her two colleagues, who walked off in the other direction, while she led us the other way down the curvy corridor. Like in the elevator, there was a rail at the side, which I grabbed hold of as I half walked, half bounced behind her.

"When nobody came, I thought the whole thing might have been a hoax," said Keya.

"Very much not," said Brimble. "But it was impossible to get word all the way out here. Not without risking discovery."

"Growing crops for human consumption using genetic properties of native plants is somewhat of a holy grail," said Keya. "We've done some experimentation here, with our limited resources, but the two domains are truly alien to each other." She pointed to the next door along. "This is the entrance to my lab up here."

She stopped and put her hand on a lockpad by the door. It opened to her palm print and revealed what appeared to be nothing – only a space half as wide as the corridor with a blank metal wall at the other side. As she stepped through, I saw the top of a ladder sticking up just above floor level. It descended into a channel large enough for a person to comfortably climb down.

I climbed onto the ladder after Keya and felt my weight increase as I stepped, rung by rung, further out from the centre of the station where the centrifugal force was stronger. By the time I got to the bottom, the gravity felt almost normal.

I stepped out into a space crammed with equipment. Benches stretched out in parallel behind each other, some with workscreens bedded into them and others with racks of test tubes and sealed flasks of chemicals. There were several machines, including a powerful microscope. Two male members of staff, both in the same white uniform, looked up from their work as Freddi and Brimble made their way down the ladder.

"Do you have it, Keya?" asked one of them.

"Is it for real?" said the other.

Keya held up the memory ball to show them. "Let's see, shall we?"

Introducing the two men as Vyan and Ishir, she went to the far end of the lab and placed the memory ball into a reader. Her colleagues clustered around her as she brought up the de-coded document. In the scientists' excitement, the three of us were all but forgotten, although I was able to stand behind and watch the same pages I had seen in Nick's workshop scroll across her screen.

"Stop – there!" said Vyan.

Keya paused and all three of them peered closer.

"This is fantastic," said Keya.

"Keep scrolling," said Ishir.

She tapped at the screen again. "Truly fantastic."

They might have stood there for hours if I had not interrupted them. "Is it what you hoped it would be?"

"I would need to study it to be sure," said Keya. "Then we will need to replicate the data, of course. But the paper appears to have been written by someone with the right scientific knowledge."

"You can use it to feed people?" asked Freddi.

"That is the hope," said Keya.

Brimble looked disappointed to the point of being upset. "Don't you know? Many people risked a lot to bring that here. I've had to leave my home forever – a friend of mine died."

Keya stepped away from the screen and turned to Brimble. I could see it hurt her to leave her holy grail. "Let me assure you, we will do everything we can. We have the best people here. I am only trying to be honest with you when I say we will need to assess the research. But, from what I have seen so far, it looks truly promising."

"How long?" said Freddi.

"To read the paper? A day. To replicate the data? Months if we're lucky; years if we're not. Until people on the Rim are able to sit down to dinner made with crops grown using the knowledge you brought with you? Within a generation, I would like to hope." She walked past the three of us towards the centre of the lab. "Follow me, I have something I'd like to show to you."

We walked down to the far end of the lab which, rather than being a wall as I had thought, was actually a row of floor to ceiling cupboards which stretched the width of the room. She pulled open a pair of double doors to reveal twenty or thirty racks of gel pods bathed in light. Growing out of them were tiny specks of rusty green.

Brimble peered in until his face was almost touching one of the gel trays. "What's that?"

"Some of our plant stocks," said Keya. "We have managed to build up a substantial collection over the years. We also have seed repositories in some of our zero-G areas. Most acquired 'surreptitiously', shall we say. We have been preparing for this opportunity for many years on Octavia. I can assure you that your friend's sacrifice will not be wasted."

She closed the cupboard again.

"Now," she said. "Is there anything I can do for you while you are here?"

"What I really need is a job," I said.

She raised her eyebrows. "Do you have a scientific background?"

"No." I laughed. "No, I'm a freelancer with a spaceship. We haven't had a paying job for a while and the last lot of repairs really put a dent in my finances. I was just wondering if you had any jobs requiring a spaceship, or maybe know someone in the system who might."

"I might be able to find something," said Keya. Not very convincingly. "I was more thinking of something that would utilise our expertise here on the station. For example, we have a medical research team if you would like someone to take a look at your nose."

Slightly embarrassed that my injury was so visible, I touched my bruised face and felt where it was still swollen. "Perhaps I should check that it isn't broken," I said.

"I'm sure my team will happily do that."

"Do you do DNA testing?" said Freddi.

I scowled at him. "Freddi!"

Keya looked pleased to be asked. "Of course we do! DNA lies at the heart of a lot of biological testing. What do you have in mind?"

Freddi pulled his scrunched up handkerchief from his trouser pocket and unravelled it to reveal the brown hair he had picked off my shoulder when he had caught me and Stephen kissing. "We want to know if the owner of this hair is related to Cassy."

Keya smiled. "Of course we can do that for you."

Chapter Twenty Six

After having had my nose scanned and prodded, and having a swab rubbed around the inside of my mouth to get a DNA sample, I found Freddi in the docking area wheeling a large crate stacked with boxes. They were all white, like the scientists' uniforms, with writing stamped on the side: '*Medical Supplies. Handle with Care*'.

"How's your nose?" he called out as I exited the elevator.

"Not broken. They put some stuff on the cut so it shouldn't leave a scar." I looked across to the crate. "What are you doing?"

"Keya found us a job," said Freddi. "Taking medical supplies to a colony in the Alfreiti system. Give me a hand, will you?"

I helped him push the crate over to our ship and leant my elbow on the top layer of boxes while we waited for the bay doors to open.

"Did you get a good price?" I asked him.

He grimaced. "Ah, that was the thing I was waiting for the right time to tell you. I may have allowed Keya to negotiate a discount. It's a bit of mercy mission, apparently. Medical emergency and all that."

I shook my head. He had no aptitude for business, which was probably why I was still the captain. "I may have to re-think that pay rise we talked about," I joked.

The ramp descended and we wheeled the crate on board. Freddi started unpacking the boxes and I joined him until the crate was empty and a corner of the cargo hold was full.

"Where's Brimble?" I asked.

"On the station somewhere," said Freddi. "He seems a bit lost. He knows he can't go back to Fertilla and he's never lived anywhere else. I think he was trying to see if he could find work here, but it seems they don't have any openings for serving tea."

I laughed. "I bet."

"We should catch up with him before we leave for Alfreiti. I know there won't be anything for him there either – it's a dismal place – but we should be able to drop him off somewhere. If we leave him, he could be stuck here for a long time before another ship comes along."

"Agreed," I said. "Are you all right taking that crate back? There's something I need to get from my room."

"Sure," he said.

I had only taken a few steps before he called after me. "Hey, Cassy, what did they say about the DNA?"

I turned. "They're going to run the test to see if me and Stephen are related. When I said I had some clothes which used to belong to King John, they said they could test them as well to help with the comparison. Apparently, some of his skin cells would have come off onto the fabric when he tried on the suit."

"Then you'll know for sure," said Freddi.

"I suppose."

"You *do* want to know, don't you?"

I shrugged. I had lied to Stephen about the code and betrayed his family by taking it to the scientists. Even though I knew I had done the right thing, it meant the chances of us being together were slim, whatever the DNA result said. "It might have been better if I had never known any of this."

"I'm sorry, Cassy. If I thought you didn't want the DNA test done, I never would have mentioned it."

"No, it's okay. I was only thinking that before all this started, I had an image of who my mother and father were. But now…" I shook my head. There was no undoing what already had been done. "I've started down this path and I need to walk to the end of it."

I turned away and went to collect my mother's box from my room.

Chapter Twenty Seven

THE SOFAS IN the recreation lounge of the Octavia Research Station looked upright and functional with their compact shape and wipe-clean surfaces, but when I sat in one and allowed my body to sink into it, the cushions hugged me like a long lost friend. A day after arriving on the ORS, I was beginning to relax and let go of the strain of everything that had happened since the Fertillan Guard first arrived on my ship.

It helped that the scientists who lived there were also relaxed. It was the only place on the station I had seen them in civilian clothes rather than their usual whites. They worked long hours, but it didn't seem to bother them because they had a purpose to their work which went beyond finding the next meal. It seemed to invigorate them.

The place was rife with people having sexual relationships of various kinds and I had seen several couples walking around with the sort of glint in their eye that suggested they were having extra-curricular activities. I had even seen two people openly kissing the night before. It was all normal. There were no children, though. It was strictly a work and recreation place.

Even Brimble seemed to have settled in in a strange way. He was somewhat of a novelty to the staff, impressing them with his connection to royalty and enthralling them with his tales of courtly life. The previous night he had engaged some of them in an impromptu class on how to bow and curtsey which they all found hysterically funny. As I sat being hugged by the sofa cushions, I could see him up the other end of the lounge sitting around a table with three others, all engaged in conversation.

Freddi sat opposite me on another one of the upright, functional, wipe-clean sofas. He wasn't letting the cushions embrace him, rather he was perched on the edge with his elbow resting on the arm while he looked at something on his P-tab. We had been discussing where we might go after the Alfreiti system and had come up with a few ideas, but no concrete plan.

Keya entered the lounge from the elevator in the middle of the far wall. A wave of calm seemed to ripple across the people as they gradually became aware of her presence. Being the one in charge, she carried with her a sense of authority that meant she was always on duty.

She caught my eye and came over. "I'm glad I found you two in here," she said.

Freddi looked up from his P-tab, saw who it was and stuffed the device in his pocket.

"Have you read the document we brought?" I asked.

"Twice," said Keya; her eyes alight with enthusiasm, coupled with the tiredness of someone who had been up half the night.

"It's… very impressive."

"So it'll work?" I said.

"It's early days, but I'm optimistic."

She must have seen Freddi's doubtful expression.

"Very optimistic," she emphasised. "Science is always a theory until it's proven, but I think we can replicate their work. Thank you for bringing it here. We would never have made this breakthrough without it."

"We should probably be leaving soon," said Freddi.

"Which is why I was looking for you," said Keya, turning to me. "Your DNA results are through. The team did a rush job on them for me."

I felt some of my tension returning. "What do they say?"

"I haven't read them yet myself. I can send a copy to your P-tab, but if you want to come to my lab, I can talk them through with you."

During the second half of her sentence, a communicator clipped to Keya's belt had been bleating. "Excuse me," she said. She yanked it free from its clip and brought it to her mouth. "Sharma!"

A female voice replied through its tinny speaker. She sounded a little panicked. "Keya, a ship's docked in Area B."

By Keya's expression, it didn't look like she was expecting it. "Who is it?"

"I don't know," the voice replied. "They didn't ask permission. They just… docked."

"I'll be right there." Keya tried to hide her concern as she clipped the communicator back onto her belt and turned apologetically to us. "I can meet you there in, say, half an hour? There's a buzzer on the lockpad, I'll make sure my staff know to let you in."

She was already walking back to the elevator.

Freddi turned to me. "Do you want me to come with you?" he said. "I understand if you want to keep the results private."

I thought about it for a moment. "No, come," I said. "If we're going to keep travelling in space together, then you should know everything."

On the way out of the recreation lounge, we stopped by the table where Brimble was sitting to mention some of the ideas we had of where we should go after we had dropped off the medical supplies. I could see that the thought frightened him. The places were just names to him, and although he nodded as we said each one, and smiled politely as we pointed out the opportunities they might be able to offer, his eyes glazed over and he wasn't really listening. We made him make a note of the list on his P-tab and left him with it.

I said nothing to Freddi as we walked over to the elevator. He was probably thinking the same as me: there would be no easy place for Brimble to settle. We would probably have to pick one for him.

The door of the elevator slid shut behind us and we were together in the small, still room.

"Where was Keya's lab again?" asked Freddi.

"Um… Level One."

Freddi spoke to the room. "Elevator, Level One."

The elevator jolted and its motors whirred. Freddi grinned to have instructed it correctly. It was a short ride and the motors soon slowed again, followed by a little bounce as it came to a halt.

I waited for the doors to open.

Nothing happened.

We looked at each other.

The strip of light which ran round the top of the walls turned to red. "Security alert," said the elevator's artificial voice, devoid of emotion. "All staff to lockdown."

Freddi looked as worried as I felt. "The ship that docked without permission?" he said.

"That's my thinking."

"We can't stay in here."

"Elevator," I instructed. "Level One."

The room responded with silence.

I tried again; more urgent this time. "Elevator, doors open!"

The door slid aside to reveal what looked to be the same curving corridor we had first entered with Keya. We had already arrived at Level One.

We stepped out into the reduced gravity environment and I felt a little sick as my gut bounced inside of me.

Coming towards us were a group of, maybe, five scientists in white. They were trying to run, but without the pull of normal strength gravity, they were half bouncing, half falling along the corridor.

"What's going on?" I called to a panicked-looking man in front.

"Soldiers," he said, breathless.

"Where?"

"On the station."

That much was obvious, but unhelpful. He went to run/bounce/fall past me, but I grabbed the lapel of his tunic and spun him back round. "Where on the station?"

"I don't know. Everywhere!" He pulled at my hand to try to free it from his clothing. "They have guns – everyone has to go to lockdown position."

I let him go.

But Freddi reached out for one of others and pulled her to the side – easy with her lesser weight. "Where are our weapons?"

She stared blankly back at him.

"Our weapons," Freddi repeated. "They took them off us when we arrived. Where are they?"

"Guns aren't allowed on Octavia," she said. "If shots breach the station, we lose pressure, we lose air."

I stepped in. "That hasn't stopped the soldiers."

"Okay," she said. I don't know if she was persuaded by my argument or was just scared by the way Freddi was holding onto her, but she led us around the corridor to one of the identical doors in its side. She put her hand on a lockpad and the door opened to reveal, not an opening with a ladder, but a cupboard with mostly empty shelves. My EEW was there, as was Freddi's knife.

As he reached in to grab it, he let go of the woman and she ran/bounced/fell back the way we had come.

Putting the knife back inside his jacket, Freddi searched the shelves and found another EEW. It was smaller and less powerful than mine, but a better defence than a fifteen-centimetre blade.

"Back to the ship?" he said.

"What about Keya?" I said. "What about Brimble?"

"We're no match for soldiers. We're going to have to hope the station's security measures keep them safe."

It was a vain hope. A bunch of scientists who banned the use of guns would be no match for armed military – if, indeed, that's what the 'soldiers' were. I wish I had taken the woman's communicator from her so we could find out what was going on. But she was long gone, disappeared somewhere along the curve.

"Back to the ship," I agreed.

There were two elevators on that corridor, one that led to the recreation area and another, on the opposite side, which led down to Docking Area A where our ship was.

We almost shot past the elevator door with the momentum and both of us had to hold onto the rail to stop ourselves. Getting his balance back, Freddi reached out for the elevator call pad, but before he could touch it, the door slid open.

A scientist in white with a petrified expression fell out into the corridor like he had been pushed from behind. That's when I saw the brown of Fertillan Guard uniforms and the black of their EE rifles.

I whipped myself back against the wall to the side of the door. Not being used to the lack of gravity, I used too much force and bounced off the wall, right in front of the first guardsman to emerge from the elevator.

We locked eyes. We saw each other's panic.

He raised his EE rifle, but my EE handgun was already pointed in his direction. I let off a poorly aimed shot and the energy blast seared into his shoulder.

He screamed as shouts came from the other guards spilling out of the elevator, and the petrified scientist was shoved out of the way.

I turned and ran as best I could, using one hand to pull myself forward as I kept my gun ready in the other.

I didn't see Freddi. He had been on the other side of the ele-vator and there were now five or six Fertillan Guard separating us.

A shot whizzed past my shoulder and I instinctively ducked as it scorched the wall by my ear. I felt the rush of air pulled from around me as it escaped into the vacuum of space beyond. Red light shone down on me and an artificial voice warned of a contamination breach as blocking foam sprayed into the hole to seal the rupture.

"Stop!" cried one of the guards. "Or the next shot won't miss!"

I had no intention of stopping. A door which must have been left open by one of the scientists in their rush to get to lockdown offered a possibility of cover.

I fired a defensive shot behind me. Three guards pushed themselves against the wall as my energy blast sailed past them and struck the curve of the floor rising up behind.

Jumping into the gap created by the open door, I stood on the top rung of the ladder and breathed heavily as I desperately tried to think of a way out.

I fired another random shot at the guards and saw they were closer. Two energy blasts whizzed past me.

I was trapped. I could close the door, lock myself in and climb down to whatever was at the bottom. But the only way out from there would be back up with the guards. If I went into the corridor, the guards would either shoot me or capture me. I needed to blast my way out and find Freddi.

I peered out to fire another shot, taking a dangerous moment to aim. But the guards were waiting. Light flashed from the muzzles of three guns. I pulled myself back in again, but my gun arm was last to find cover and energy struck the barrel with such force that it was knocked from my hand and my gun went tumbling down the corridor.

I cried out with the pain of it being wrenched from my grip and the terror of being suddenly unarmed.

I frantically started to climb down the ladder. I pulled at the door to lock it shut behind me, but it was yanked from my grasp.

A guard stood at the open door and pointed his EE rifle at my head.

"Come out!" he ordered.

I was still climbing.

"Or I shoot you," he said.

I stopped. The terror of defeat clawed at my throat. I clung onto the ladder like I was clinging to the last little bit of my freedom.

"Out! Now!"

I didn't want to die. I wanted to live for another opportunity to escape. So I began to climb, slowly, back to the top.

Two rungs away, a hand reached in, grabbed my jacket and pulled me out.

My body was pressed against the wall as my arms were pulled behind me and handcuffs secured to my wrists.

When I was turned back round, I saw Freddi being led down the corridor by three other guards. He, too, had his hands shackled behind him and his head bowed in defeat.

Chapter Twenty Eight

THEY WERE HOLDING everyone in the recreation lounge.

As the elevator doors opened and I was pushed into the room with my hands cuffed behind me, I saw with despair the number of people who were sitting on the floor with EE rifles trained on them by Fertillan Guards. It was more than had been relaxing, chatting and laughing in there only the previous night. It had to be most of the station. They all stared at me with terrified eyes as a gun barrel prodded me in the back and I was steered away from them to the other side of the room.

The sofa I had been sitting on less than hour before had been cleared away to the wall, along with the others, leaving an empty space where I was told to sit cross-legged. I obeyed, although it was hard to sit on the floor with my hands behind me.

It wasn't long before the elevator made a second trip and Freddi was pushed out at gunpoint. He was ordered to sit near me, but not close enough for us to speak without being overheard.

"Are you okay, Cassy?" he asked.

"Yeah," I said. "You?"

"Never better," he lied.

The guard who had brought him in the elevator swung the barrel of his gun and smashed it into Freddi's face. "No talking!" he bellowed.

Freddi was knocked sideways with the force of the blow. As he pulled himself back upright, I saw a line of blood form on his cheek.

I sat, resting back on my hands, and tried to figure out what the vac had happened. There was no way the Fertillan Guard could have tracked us to Octavia, *no way*. Nanci had got rid of the tracker they'd placed on my ship and, anyway, they couldn't have followed us through the wormhole. It didn't make sense.

All of which was irrelevant to my immediate problem, which was getting myself, Freddi and Brimble off Octavia Research Station alive and free. Looking at the number of armed guards in the room with me, it seemed like the chances of doing that were near to zero. My only bargaining chip was my relationship with their Prince Stephen, but I had lied to him about the code and betrayed his family to bring it to the scientists, so that chip was massively devalued, if it had any value left in it at all.

I looked around at the room to assess the resources available to me. The contingent of Fertillan Guards kept changing as some came and some went, but there were approximately six of them at any one time. Freddi and I were handcuffed and closely watched, but the scientists had their hands free and there were a lot more scientists than guards. Whether any of them had the ability to fight was another matter, and getting any messages to them was nigh-on impossible as we were separated both by several metres and by armed guards. I noticed Brimble was sitting among them, although I doubted he could be of any more use than they were.

My mind kept turning over, treading the same old ground with no solution and so I didn't notice yet another arrival of the elevator. It was only Freddi clearing his throat that made me look up.

He mouthed something at me that I couldn't read. I stared harder as he repeated it: *Trevel.*

Standing by the elevator door, talking in a whisper to one of the guards, was a man whose face was chillingly familiar. Freddi was right, it was Trevel, Prince Stephen's right-hand man.

There was movement among the scientists. The guard watching them reacted by lifting his rifle as, to my horror, Brimble stood up. He looked small, thin and vulnerable.

"Sit down!" barked the guard.

Brimble did not. Instead he bravely – foolishly – called out. "Lieutenant Trevel!"

Trevel spun to face him. Brimble visibly jumped as the guard pointed his rifle. "Shut up and sit down!"

Trevel held up his hand to quieten the guard. He peered at Brimble, looking intently into his face as he stepped closer. "I know you," he said. "You work at Londos House."

"This is an independent research station," said Brimble. "The Fertillan Guard has no jurisdiction."

"Then you shouldn't have brought us here."

"Me?"

"Or maybe you shouldn't have told Andrus Hoggard's widow where you were going," said Trevel. "Mothers with babies will do anything to protect their child."

Brimble's eyes widened with realisation. His face reddened with anger. *"You–"*

The swear word didn't come as Trevel pulled an EEW from his belt and aimed it right between Brimble's eyes. I thought he was actually going to shoot him.

"Hey, Trevel!" I called out.

Freddi glared at me: *Cassy, no!* he mouthed.

I had Trevel's attention. Behind him, I saw scientists pulling Brimble back down to the floor.

"Yeah, Trevel, remember me?"

I saw the recognition in his face as he forgot Brimble and came towards me; each step of his military boots tapping on the hard floor.

He glared at me with distain. "Individual Sesaan Cassandra. I was going to say it is a surprise to see you, but that wouldn't be the case."

I struggled to stand up. It was hard because, with my hands behind me, I had nothing to push me up from the floor and my body was unbalanced. He watched with amusement as I knelt and then staggered to my feet.

"Does Prince Stephen know you're doing this?" I said, once my eyes were almost at the level of his.

"It was Marshal Commander Regellan who ordered it," said Trevel.

I didn't know if I was relieved Stephen might be there or scared he had already forsaken me. "I want to see him," I said. "I demand to see him!"

"You," said Trevel, putting his hand on my shoulder. "Are not in the position to demand anything."

He pushed me back so hard that I stumbled. Without my hands free, I went crashing down on the floor and landed hard on my side. I lay there for moment and listened to Trevel's retreating footsteps.

"Cassy, what the hell are you doing?" It was Freddi's voice, but I couldn't see him from where I was lying.

"No talking!" bellowed the same guard who had hit Freddi in the face.

But this time, he didn't hit anyone. Our resulting silence was enough.

Ten minutes later, the elevator brought more bad news. A Fertillan Guard arrived dragging an exhausted and reluctant Keya Sharma. I dreaded to think what sort of fight she had put up as strands of her plait had come loose and were hanging around her face in a tangled mess. Her make-up had smudged to leave dark circles around the eyes and she was barely keeping herself upright. She, too, had her hands cuffed behind her back.

"Lieutenant Trevel," said the guard with puffed-up pride. "This is the one in charge."

Trevel nodded at the news, as if it was nothing less than he expected. "Put her in the middle where I can see her, well away from the others."

Keya was dumped on the floor like the rest of us, equidistant between her staff and Freddi and me.

That was it, then. That was all of us. Captured and helpless.

Chapter Twenty Nine

THERE WAS BARELY a trace of the Prince Stephen I knew as he came into the recreation lounge. In his Fertillan Guard uniform, with his hat pressed down on his head so it shaded his eyes, he was entirely Marshal Commander Regellan. I forgot why I had ever found him attractive.

"Stephen!" I shouted.

He turned to look at me just as the guard who had us at gunpoint swung the barrel of his rifle across my face. I heard the crack of the metal strike my teeth through my cheek as much as I felt the pain of it as I was knocked sideways onto the floor. "Quiet!" he bellowed.

When I pulled myself back up to sitting, Stephen was no longer looking in my direction. He was talking to Trevel. They spoke in hushed tones for many minutes. It was as if I didn't exist.

I looked to Freddi who was still sitting a little way from me, but he could offer no help. Only a sympathetic look.

Stephen finished his conversation with Trevel and paced into the centre of the recreation lounge. He looked around at the assembled crowd like a politician about to make a speech. I tried to return his gaze, to find some recognition – some sliver of humanity – but he looked straight through me. "Many of you will know who I am," he said. "But many others of you are from worlds or colonies a long way from Fertilla, and so I will tell you that I am Marshal Commander Regellan of the Fertillan Guard. My other title is Prince Stephen Regellan, brother to King Richard of Fertilla. I am here because of the theft of a document from my family. A document that was brought here, to your research station, a document of a highly confidential and dangerous nature. Ordinarily, my authority would not reach out this far, but this is a case of exceptional interstellar espionage."

He paced. Laying down his authority with each step as he walked back and forth in front of his captive audience. "I have no desire to harm you in any way. I am merely here to destroy the document. My guardsmen and women will be infiltrating all your computers and electronic devices to purge every trace of its existence."

"You can't do that!" I blurted out.

He spun on his heel and turned to face me. This time he looked me in the eye. I searched his face for a hint of the man who had kissed me so tenderly in his conservatory, and so passionately in Mandi's house, but if it still existed, then he hid it very well.

"I can do it, and I will."

"But the knowledge will be dead and gone!" I said. "The knowledge that could help so many people. *Stephen, please!* If I know you at all, then I know you're not the sort of man who would sacrifice the welfare of people on the Rim for your own wealth and power."

I saw the confusion in his eyes for a fleeting moment before I felt the guard's gun in my face again and tasted the blood from a loosened back molar.

"It's true!" said Keya.

I sat back up again to see Stephen standing over her and glaring down at where she had been made to sit cross-legged on the floor. "Who are you?"

"Doctor Keya Sharma, Your Highness. I run this station."

"If you are worried about your personnel, Doctor, then be assured that I have no interest in harming them. As long as they do not obstruct my operation, then they have nothing to fear."

"But the document–"

"Is not yours," he concluded.

Stephen spun round to face Trevel. "Trevel!"

Trevel brought his heels to attention. "Sire."

Stephen pointed a finger at Keya. "Keep this one quiet." Then he pointed directly at me. "Bring this woman to my room."

"Yes, Sire."

"And wait to purge the computers until my direct and express order."

"But, Sire–" began Trevel.

"Don't 'but, Sire' me, just do it!"

"Yes, Sire. Of course, Sire."

Stephen stepped towards the elevator and disappeared behind its sliding door.

On Trevel's orders, the guard with both my and Freddi's blood on the barrel of his gun, grabbed my arm and pulled me to standing. He marched me to the elevator, bundled me inside and took me to Stephen's ship.

Chapter Thirty

I WAS TAKEN DIRECTLY to Stephen's private office, where he sat, throne-like, on a large impressive chair with his elbows resting on the desk in front of him and his fingers interlocked to form a bridge where he rested his chin. The office was a generous size for a spaceship, yet he commanded it naturally. From the large screen embedded into the desk, to the many pictures on the walls showing his family and idealised scenes of Fertilla.

"The woman, Commander," said the guard, as he pushed me inside. The man had clearly taken no note of my name and had made no effort to ask what it was as he manhandled me over.

"Put her in the chair," said Stephen.

There was a single chair opposite his desk which I got forcibly shoved down into, as if I didn't know how to sit on it without help. I perched on the edge as my arms, still restrained behind me, wouldn't allow me to sit back properly.

"That will be all," said Stephen.

The guard hesitated.

Stephen frowned at him. "She's three quarters my size and handcuffed, for the Deity's sake! I don't see her as a threat, do you?"

"No, Commander," said the guard. "Of course, not, Commander." He stood to attention for a moment, then marched out and closed the door behind him.

I was alone with Stephen. I wriggled my wrists in the cuffs and tried to keep the blood flowing to my hands. The metal was cutting into my skin and hurting from where it had been bruised by Brimble's friends on the night of the ambush.

"Well, Cassy," said Stephen. "This is your one chance to explain yourself."

"You can't destroy the document," I began. "It's too important. Talk to Keya, talk to Brimble, they'll tell you–"

He held up his hand to stop me. "To explain why you lied to me. Why you conspired with a member of my staff. Why you took something that belonged to my family and gave it to a bunch of outcasts living out here on the edge of the Rim. Not to mention, Cassy, why you ran away from Fertilla without telling me."

"I didn't mean to deceive you," I said. I was about to go through the whole story. But none of that mattered any longer. I paused, trying to think of the right words. It was, as he said, my one chance to explain. "Remember when I asked you in the car what was it that Hoggard stole? You said you couldn't tell me, even if you knew."

"That is what I said."

"That was true, wasn't it? You didn't know. You still don't know."

Stephen shrugged. "Family secrets. Security details that could be disastrous if they fall into the wrong hands. James–"

"Prince James didn't tell you it was a scientific document, am I right? That's why we brought it here, to a science research station. If there's a family secret, it's that James didn't want other people to know the research existed. If there's a security concern, it's because the document details how native plants from Fertilla can be used to grow food for everyone on the Rim. But I remember how excited you were in your conservatory when you showed me the plants growing on the planet's surface. If you're the man I think you are, you'll want to preserve this science for the good of everyone, not be the one who has it destroyed."

He sat back in his chair and waved his hands dismissively. "That science is impossible. People proved that over a generation ago."

"Maybe they didn't. Maybe they proved the opposite and the result was suppressed. If you don't believe me, ask Doctor Keya Sharma. At the very least, save the research contained in that document. If it turns out to be impossible, then nothing has been lost. But if you destroy it, the knowledge will be lost forever."

He rocked in his chair. He brought his hands to his chin and rubbed his fingertips along the stubble which had grown there. "Why should I believe you over my own brother?"

"You don't have to believe me. Would it be enough to give me the benefit of the doubt? Let Keya show you, so you can see for yourself. She can take you to the research she's carrying out in her lab, she can show you the document and explain what it means – far better than a non-scientist like me."

Stephen nodded. "Okay."

"Okay?" I repeated. "You will?"

He stood.

"I brought you in here because I genuinely wanted to know what you had to say. So I will see this doctor woman, as you suggest, then I shall be in a position to make up my own mind."

He walked over to the door and turned the handle.

"What about me?" I said, fearing he was going to walk off.

"I'll get someone to put you in the cells while I decide what to do with you. Regardless of your motives, you've still committed a criminal offence. Several, if I'm not mistaken."

"No! You need to take me with you. Just let me out of these cuffs and I'll be no trouble." I lifted up my arms as much as I could behind me to indicate my aching, shackled wrists.

"I can't," said Stephen.

"You can trust me, I swear."

"I meant, I haven't got a key."

"*Please*, Stephen, don't lock me in a cell."

He flung open the door and I thought he was going to leave me. But he sighed and seemed to change his mind. He stepped back into the office, took me by the arm and pulled me to my feet. "I'll find someone with a key on the way over," he said. "Do you know your trouble, Individual Sesaan Cassandra?"

"My trouble?" I said.

"You haven't learnt to say, 'yes, Sire.'"

Together we walked, with me half stumbling by his side, back into the heart of the space station.

Chapter Thirty One

THE ELEVATOR SHUDDERED and came to a halt so suddenly that it sent me crashing against the side wall. The strip light near the ceiling flipped from white to red.

The elevator spoke in its customary dispassionate manner. "Containment breach detected."

I looked across to Stephen who had grabbed onto the rail much easier than I could with my cuffed hands. He wasn't looking at me, he was looking up at the light.

"Elevator?" I called out. "What's going on?"

"Safety procedures activated," it replied.

Stephen looked across to me with a worried expression. "That felt like an explosion somewhere on the station," he said.

It felt like it to me, too.

The elevator spoke again: "Station integrity restored. Elevator operation resuming."

There was a gentle jolt and the sound of motors whirring as the room continued its journey.

It bounced a little as it came to a stop and the door slid open to reveal the opposite wall of a curved corridor and a man in white lying sprawled on the floor. The scorch mark from an EEW was burned into his chest and the white of his tunic had been turned almost entirely into red from his blood. The paleness of his skin and the unblinking milkiness of his eyes only confirmed he was long dead.

Stephen stepped out over the body. I followed.

There was another scorch mark on the wall beside the lift and, within the hole it had made, the solidified, white mass of hardened blocking foam.

Ignoring the evidence of whatever fight had happened there, Stephen took my arm with one hand and grabbed the rail with the other hand, as he led us in a hopping walk towards the other elevator which would take us to Keya in the recreation lounge.

A group of three Fertillan Guards – pushing a terrified-looking scientist with a tear down the front of her tunic – came into view heading towards us.

I tensed, even though I was in Stephen's custody.

"Guardsman!" shouted Stephen. "What's going on? What are you doing with this woman?"

The lead guardsman halted abruptly and stood to attention. The other two fell in behind him. The forward motion of the scientist's body caused her to drift towards us until her captor pulled her back and her feet touched the floor again.

"We can't take weapons in the elevators unless we have authorisation from one of the station staff," the guard explained.

Stephen frowned and stared closely at the guardsman's insignia on his uniform. "Then let me relieve you of your weapon, Sergeant. Give me your sidearm."

"Yes, Commander." Flustered, the man reached for his holster, pulled out his military-grade EE handgun and passed it to Stephen.

Stephen felt the weight of it in his hand. "Do you have the key to unlock these handcuffs?" He gestured down at my secured hands.

"Commander?"

Stephen clicked his fingers three times in succession. "Key! Key! Key!"

The sergeant fumbled in his pocket and handed an electronic key to his superior officer.

The corridor shook and all of us lurched to one side.

A red light radiated from above, followed by an emotionless voice. "Containment breach detected. Safety protocol Gamma."

"What's safety protocol Gamma?" Stephen demanded.

He was asking the hapless guardsman in front of him, but it was the scientist who answered. "It's a breach in one of the outer modules," she said. "It means there's minimal risk to the main hub of the station, but we have to stay in our positions until given the all-clear."

"Commander," said the sergeant. "Lieutenant Trevel says the scientists have rigged this place to blow. We've been ordered to evacuate."

The red glow around us changed back to white. "Station integrity restored. Safety protocols rescinded. Access to Level Twelve for maintenance teams only."

"May I have your permission to continue, Commander?" said the sergeant.

"Permission granted," said Stephen.

The guards hurried off down the corridor, taking the scientist with them.

I looked at Stephen in disbelief. "What about her?"

"Sounds like she'll be safer in custody on my ship than if they let her go."

He held up the key he had taken from the sergeant and gestured for me to turn round. I turned my back to him and heard the clicks of the handcuff locks release. It was an amazing relief as I was able – finally – to bring my arms in front of me. The cuffs clattered to the floor and I kicked them away as I rubbed my sore and bruised wrists; encouraging more blood to flow into my cold, blue-tinged fingers.

"I can't believe Keya would initiate any sort of self-destruct," I said. "The station is carrying out a lot of important research – not just the Fertillan stuff – some of it is medical research."

Stephen glanced at me, doubtfully. "And none of it is the slightest bit illicit? Out here on the edge of the Rim where few people are going to come snooping?" He pulled his communicator from his pocket and shouted into it. "Trevel?"

We waited. There was no reply.

"Trevel!" Still nothing. "Trevel, this is Marshal Commander Regellan – report!" He waited again. "Someone – anyone – report."

A female voice responded. "This is Second Lieutenant Vanston, Commander. Evacuation is almost complete. Station staff have been locked in the recreation lounge, as per your orders."

"My orders?" he questioned.

"Yes, Commander," she said.

"I ordered no such thing. Lieutenant, when you find Trevel, tell him to get his head out of his arse and contact me."

"Yes, Comm–"

He took his finger off the communicator and cut her off mid-word.

"We need to get Keya and Freddi and all the scientists out of the recreation lounge," I said.

"What about the small matter of the space station exploding?" said Stephen.

"Then we need to do it quickly." I grabbed at the rail with my liberated hands and pulled myself along as I ran/hopped to the elevator.

When I got there, the door was already open. I stepped in.

Moments behind, Stephen came in after me. "I'm going to regret not putting you in that cell, aren't I?" he said.

"Probably."

I grabbed the rail, but the elevator seemed inert. Every other time I had ridden in one in the station, the door had closed automatically once I was inside. "Elevator!" I called to the room. "Recreation lounge." Nothing happened. "Recreation lounge. Authorisation Sharma. Elevator respond!"

"Perhaps it's my EEW," said Stephen, holding up the sidearm he had taken from the sergeant.

"Except the elevator would say that it had detected a weapon," I said. "Unless… wait here."

I jumped out of the elevator and grabbed at the rail in the corridor as I bounced in the reduced gravity.

"Cassy!" Stephen called out behind me.

But I was already rushing back the way we had come, remembering how Keya had instructed the elevator to proceed when we brought weapons on board and knowing that she held the highest authority on the station. If the only way out of the recreation lounge was via the elevator, and if it had been locked to prevent the staff from escaping, then there was a chance Keya could unlock it. If the system was still in working order.

I apologised to the dead man outside the other elevator as I unclipped the communicator from his belt and took it back to where Stephen was waiting for me, standing in the corridor with his arms folded.

I bounced past him and in through the open door. "I hope this works," I said, as he followed me in for the second time. "I don't fancy having to climb along the elevator shaft to get to them."

The communicator was a simple lightweight device which I held easily in my palm. Its only controls were a single button which sat alongside an indicator light, a speaker and a microphone. Person-to-person communication was probably directed via use of a verbal code. A code which I didn't know. So I pressed the button and spoke into the microphone using every possible keyword I could think of. "Call to Doctor Keya Sharma. Put me through to Doctor Keya Sharma. Come in, Doctor Keya Sharma."

One of them must have worked because it bleated the same ringing tone – just quieter and at a lower pitch – as the one emitted by Keya's communicator in the recreation lounge. I waited for her to answer. Stephen looked at me; I looked at Stephen. The longer we waited, the more I feared her communicator had been taken from her and was ringing unheard somewhere in a Fertillan Guard stockpile.

Assuming Keya hadn't been incapacitated, or even killed.

The ringing stopped. "Hello?" came a voice through the speaker.

"Keya? It's Cassy – Sesaan Cassandra. Are you okay? Where are you?"

"We're fine," she said. It was definitely her. "The Fertillan Guard have all gone, but they've locked us in the recreation lounge and shot out the elevator controls. If we can't call the elevator, we can't get out. Some of the others are trying to pull panels off the wall to get to the shaft."

"I'm in the elevator now, Keya. It looks to be in working order, but it's locked somehow. I'm hoping you can override it with voice activation. Can you do that?"

"Over the communicator?" she responded.

"Yeah. Is there a way to turn up the volume?"

"You say: communicator, maximum volume."

"Oh." That was sort of obvious. "Communicator, maximum volume." I paused. "Go ahead, Keya."

"Elevator," came Keya's voice. It was a little louder, although not massively so. "Release lock: authorisation Sharma. Elevator, recreation lounge."

The elevator did nothing. It made no sound. The door stayed open.

Stephen took the communicator from my hand.

"What are you doing?"

He made no reply as he held the device up to the ceiling and nearer to a receptor which I hadn't even noticed.

"Try again, Doctor," he called.

"Elevator, release lock: authorisation Sharma," came her voice. "Elevator, recreation lounge."

I sighed with relief as the door slid shut. But the elevator did not move. The strip light turned from white to red.

The elevator spoke. "One EE weapon detected."

It meant it was working. It was actually working.

Keya's voice came again: "Elevator, authorisation Sharma to proceed to recreation lounge with one EEW present."

The elevator jolted, the motors whirred and we were on our way.

CHAPTER THIRTY TWO

A MASSIVE CHEER GREETED us as the elevator arrived in the recreation lounge and the door slid open.

A cheer that suddenly trickled to a halt as the scientific staff saw Stephen was in there with me. He raised his EEW and walked forward.

They backed away from him like repelled particles and created a clear path through their human bodies as he headed into the centre of the room. I matched his steps as, behind me, the first part of the crowd rushed into the now-working elevator.

"Cassy!" It was Freddi's voice.

I spun around, looking for him.

He came running up to me, his hands still in cuffs behind him. "Thank the Deity!"

"Are you okay, Freddi?"

"Better now that you're here."

Stephen stepped up behind me. He held out the key he had

taken from the sergeant. "Do you want to be free of those?" he said, nodding at Freddi's restrained arms.

"The vac do I!"

"Turn round," said Stephen. Freddi did as he was told. "The correct response is, 'yes, Sire.'"

But Stephen unlocked Freddi's handcuffs without further comment. The restraints clattered to the ground and Freddi let out the most enormous sigh of relief to the point of it sounding almost sexual.

The sound of an explosion rumbled through the station: distant enough not to blast a hole in the fabric of the room, but close enough to feel it. The floor beneath our feet shuddered. Some of the scientists crowded by the elevator screamed. A couple of them fell over.

"That was a close one," Freddi said.

Red light flooded the recreation lounge and the dispassionate voice spoke. "Containment breach detected," it said, barely audible above the shouts from the increasingly panicked scientists.

"Where's this Doctor Sharma I came all the way back here to see?" said Stephen.

Freddi nodded over to the crowd. Keya was standing, still handcuffed, with her back facing us while she tried to tell her staff to make an orderly exit to the survival pods. "Don't forget to send the elevator back," she urged. "Remember, we can't call it from here."

"I'll get her," said Freddi.

He touched her gently on the arm and beckoned her over to where Stephen was standing beside me.

Her hair was still a mess from where much of it had come loose from her plait, but the look of defeat was gone. There was a defiance about her, even as she stood before the man in Fertillan Guard uniform with his EEW drawn.

The flood of red light blinked out and normal white light returned. "Station integrity restored," said the voice.

"What are you doing to my station?" Keya demanded of Stephen.

"I am not the one who initiated a self-destruct sequence," he told her.

"We have no self-destruct capability on this station," she said. "Even if we did, why would I destroy years of hard work? Irreplaceable biological samples? Risk the lives of my staff?"

"Because you want to keep secret what you are doing here at all costs."

Freddi interrupted. "Does it matter who's doing it? The space station is exploding around us and we need to escape before we're either blown to pieces or a containment breach sucks us out into the vacuum. Neither is a pleasant way to die."

I had to agree with Freddi. "We have to get back to the ship." I looked around at the crowd by the elevator. It had shrunk a little, but not enough to get inside without queue jumping past a lot of increasingly desperate people.

"Freddi says you might help us because of your relationship with Cassy," said Keya.

My cheeks went hot.

Stephen didn't allow any emotion to show on his face. "Turn around," he told her.

She remained standing exactly how she was.

"I said, turn around." He grabbed her left shoulder and turned her himself so she faced away from him. He brought out the key and unlocked her handcuffs, speaking quietly in her ear as he did so. "I am prepared to give you benefit of the doubt, that's all you need to know."

The cuffs clattered to the floor and Keya turned back round, rubbing her wrists without the drama Freddi had shown. "Thank you," she said, begrudgingly.

Stephen looked across at the lessening, but still substantial crowd. He marched over there. "Out of my way!"

No one moved. A few turned to look at him, then looked quickly away.

"I said, out of my way!" he shouted and pointed his weapon towards the ceiling. He fired and energy seared its way through the fabric of the station.

People screamed as the red light descended and the voice told everyone about the containment breach they had just witnessed. Above Stephen's head, blocking foam hissed its way into the blast hole to form a seal.

"Is he mad?" said Keya. "He's going to get us all killed."

Stephen lowered his weapon and pointed it at the terrified people in front of him. They parted, like before, and formed a clear path to the elevator.

"You three!" Stephen ordered, and beckoned us forward with his gun.

Keya stood fast. "I'm not going before my people."

"The longer you stand there, the longer your people will have to wait." Stephen aimed the gun at her. "Or would you prefer I shoot you?"

Freddi tugged at her arm and reluctantly she came with us.

I tried not to look in the faces of all the innocent scientists as I walked past them, but still I felt their despising gaze pressing in on me.

We entered the elevator, Keya gave authorisation for it to proceed with Stephen's EEW on board, and we arrived back at Level One. As soon as we stepped out, the sound of little bits of *something* rattled on the other side of the wall, as if a handful of children's marbles had been dropped onto its outer surface.

"What's that?" said Keya.

"Debris from the explosions," said Stephen. "Pray there aren't any big sharp bits."

Keya sent the elevator back to the recreation lounge and we pressed ahead down the corridor. One further explosion shook us on the short trip. The voice told us the breach had been contained and that only maintenance teams were allowed beyond Level Four.

"Getting closer," Keya breathed.

I was relieved to reach the other elevator and find the enclosed room was already there waiting for us. Stephen and Keya were the first to step in.

I had one foot inside when Freddi nudged my arm. "Cassy, look, there's Brimble."

My gaze followed his pointing finger to where Brimble and a scientist – Vyan, who had been in Keya's lab when she first looked at the document – were hurrying in our direction. "Brimble, what are you doing?" I called out.

"Brimble?" I heard Stephen say behind me.

Shortly followed by Keya. "We have to go now!"

Brimble tried to go even faster when he saw me, as difficult as it was in reduced gravity with his feet bounding off the floor. He was pulling at the rail with one hand while, in the other, he held out the silver sphere of the memory ball to show me. "Cassy! I have the code! It's safe from the computer purge. One of the scientists let me into–"

The screeching of metal on metal sent shock waves up and down the corridor as a shard of station debris sliced through the ceiling behind Brimble. The jagged point speared Vyan's head and sprayed globules of his blood against the wall. The scientist opened his mouth to cry out, but the metal pierced his brain and silenced him before the scream left his lungs.

Red light everywhere.

Brimble mouthed my name, but I heard nothing as the air rushed past me and out through the breach into the vacuum of space. The memory ball slipped from his hand and was sucked through the hole with it. Brimble desperately clung to the rail, but his grip was not as strong as the vacuum's hunger. His fingers slipped and he was pulled up to the breach with his arms and legs flailing uselessly.

He was stuck, half in and half out of the station, causing the wind to slow while his body plugged the gap. But the pressure was too great and the whole section of the wall gave way – spinning out into space. One moment there was the wall and Brimble: the next there was only black.

A section containment door slammed down from the ceiling like a guillotine and severed the corridor.

The wind stopped. I gasped at the thin air. Hands – I don't know whose – pulled me inside the elevator and the door slid shut behind me.

Chapter Thirty Three

KEYA HAD TO authorise a series of overrides before she could get the elevator to take us down to Docking Area A where my ship was waiting. Stephen said we should all go back to his ship, but no one was listening to him.

The elevator door slid open to reveal the glorious sight of my ship standing tall and proud in front of us. She was ageing, battered and patched up, but she was mine and she was our way out of there.

Freddi opened the bay doors and I jumped up onto the ramp as it was still lowering.

"Ship, start the engines!" I called out.

"Where are we going, Cassy?" said Ship.

"As fast and as far away from this space station as we can."

I RAN TO the control room with Freddi at my side and the sound of Stephen and Keya's footsteps following behind.

I went straight to my position at the captain's console and Freddi took up his position at the next station.

The ship had already guided itself out of the docking area on its own. Freddi took over and steered a course past the debris field into clear space.

A blast from somewhere outside rocked us and I held onto my console to stop myself from falling over. I brought up a live image of the station on my screen and saw the aftermath of a massive explosion. What had once been a majestic, turning space station with solar panels glinting in the glow from Octavia's red giant sun, was now a mass of tumbling debris. The remnants of where people had lived, worked and made love spun away from the detonation site as dying flames ate up the last of the station's oxygen.

Keya rushed to one of the vacant consoles and watched it all unfold in a deathly silence. Until the reality of what she was seeing became part of her.

"Nooooo!" she screamed. She bashed at the screen with angry, child-like fists. "No! No! No! No!" She leant forward and put her hands around the whole console, hugging it close to her as the tears came: loud and desperate and inconsolable.

Stephen prised her off the console and took her to the side. She crumbled to the floor and sobbed. He tried to put a comforting arm around her shoulders, but she shook him free and buried her head in her knees as she hugged them close to her chest.

Freddi put extra power into the engines and we pulled away until the sound of debris hitting the hull reduced to nothing.

Chapter Thirty Four

I WENT BACK TO my room to change out of my dirty clothes.
I needed a wash, a sleep and a meal as well, but they had to
wait.

I sat on my bed to take off my boots and suddenly found I
couldn't move.

The horror of what I had witnessed paralysed me.

So many people.

So much destruction.

The realisation collapsed in on me all at once. My hands were
shaking. My muscles were jelly.

The memory of Brimble appeared in my mind as clear as
if he were standing in front of me. I saw his excited face as he
held out the memory ball like an eager child. Excitement that
turned to terror as the vacuum snatched it from his hand and
claimed his body for its own. He must have known what was coming in the moments before he was torn out of the space station.

Nothingness all around him as he gasped for air that wasn't there while every liquid molecule in his body crystallised into ice.

Brimble was dead. Vyan, who had taken him to the lab instead of heading straight for a survival pod, was dead. The scientist lying shot outside the elevator was dead. Countless others whose names I didn't know were dead. Either massacred in the recreation lounge when the station exploded or killed on their way to escape.

A carnage of horror that I was responsible for. I had brought the code to their remote scientific outpost and, with it, I had brought death.

I remembered another dead face. The face of Andrus Hoggard who had dragged me into the whole mess. I should have never listened to his dying message. The only message I should have listened to was the one conveyed by the knife in his back.

Freddi's voice came over the speakers and interrupted my thoughts. "Cassy, the Fertillan Guard ship is trying to talk to us. What do you want me to do?"

I was snapped back to the moment. I became, again, the captain of my ship. "Answer them," I said. "Confirm we have their Marshal Commander safely on board and let Stephen talk to them – but monitor what he says."

"Will do," said Freddi. The communication cut off.

I took off my boots and rubbed at my aching feet. I pulled off my socks and removed my jacket. I stepped out of my trousers and my P-tab fell from my pocket.

I stooped to pick it up and was about to put it on the side when I saw there was a message waiting for me. I somehow found myself opening it out of habit.

The heading said: *DNA results on Individual Sesaan Cassandra, Prince Stephen Regellan (presumed) and King John Regellan (presumed).*

I had forgotten all about that.

In the light of everything that had happened, it seemed trivial. Unimportant.

But I read on.

Summary of results. DNA profile for Individual Sesaan Cassandra: No familial match to Prince Stephen Regellan (presumed) and King John Regellan (presumed).

So, that was it. Days of worry dismissed with one simple sentence.

King John was not my father. Prince Stephen was not my brother.

I should have been relieved. It meant there was no genetic barrier to me and Stephen being together. It also meant I had no connection to the Regellan royal family and I could wormhole light years away from them without a second thought if I wanted.

Underneath the first result was a second statement. I had to read it twice to make sure I had understood it correctly:

DNA analysis of profiles for Prince Stephen Regellan (presumed) and King John Regellan (presumed): familial match confirmed; paternity match negative.

Paternity match negative?

But Prince Stephen *was* King John's son. That was a fact.

A fact disputed by the science.

I read it again. John and Stephen were related, but they were not father and son.

Then who was his father?

There was more detail about the scientific tests underneath the summary, but as I went to read it, the display blinked out. I tapped the screen and nothing happened. I thought perhaps it had run out of power until I saw the power indicator light was still on.

A knock on the door was so loud and sudden that I almost dropped the P-tab.

I put it on the side. "Who is it?"

"It's Stephen," came his muffled voice.

"Drakh!" I was half undressed. "Just a minute!"

I climbed back into the trousers I was planning to change out of and opened the door, a little breathless.

Stephen looked tired. The events of the last few hours seemed to have aged him. He had undone the top two buttons of his uniform jacket and several chest hairs were visible at his throat.

"I could have used the communications system, but I wanted to tell you in person," he said.

"Tell me what?"

"I've instructed my ship to pick up any survivors from the station. A number of survival pods made it out."

"That's good," I said. "But we should do that. The scientists should come here, not to a Fertillan Guard ship."

"With respect, Cassy, you do not have the resources to carry out the operation. We do. Those survival pods will only keep them alive for a matter of hours."

I hated that he was right. "I suppose."

"I will need to return to my ship to restore command. Once all the pods are on board, they'll send over a transport."

"No!" I said. "I don't want any more Fertillan Guard vessels docking with my ship."

"I need to get over there, Cassy. It's my duty."

"Then you can take our shuttle. We at least have the resources to do that."

"If that is what you prefer."

"It is."

I don't know what it was about that moment, in the tit for tat of discussion about ship resources, that made me want to kiss him, but I let the impulse rule me. I reached up with my lips and felt the warm softness of his mouth press against mine.

I stepped back; flushed with embarrassment at my impromptu move. "I'm sorry, I don't know why I did that."

"Don't be sorry," he said. "Can I come in?"

I let go of the door and allowed him in. As he stepped inside, he leant forward to kiss me. I returned the kiss. Longer this time. Sensual. Urgent.

I let my desire break free as his mouth explored mine and our lips and tongues became one. I reached around his back and pulled him closer to me, desperate for the human connection. His arm gripped round my waist and we stumbled further inside.

He kicked the door closed with his foot and, as our lips parted, we took a moment to breathe deeply with our foreheads touching each other. Breathing in the scent of each other. His scent flowed down into my lungs where it mingled with my blood and made my heart beat faster.

I reached for the buttons on his jacket and undid each one; my fingers fumbling as they struggled with the thick material. I expected to find his skin underneath, but discovered a collarless undershirt.

"So many layers," I breathed.

"They all come off." He pulled his arms out of the sleeves of the jacket and discarded it behind him.

He reached for my shirt. With one hand cupping my breast, he used the other to slip the first button out of its button hole. The second button followed. With no more patience for the other buttons, he tugged at the material and, together, we pulled my shirt off over my head.

He kissed me again. His hands explored the smooth ovals of my breasts, and my body surged with anticipation. I pulled at his shirt to bring him closer to me. He ripped it off over his head and, at last, his naked chest was next to mine. I touched the soft hairs that grew there and smiled at how they spun little dark spirals across his muscles. My fingers traced a line through their curls as I drew my fingertips across the bumps of his ribs, down his stomach and to the buckle of his belt.

My hand drifted lower to the hard, warm bulge beneath. It responded to my touch. He sighed and I knew I had signalled that I wanted his body as much as his body wanted mine.

We disposed of our remaining clothes. Fastenings ripped open. Fabric kicked away.

We pulled each other's nakedness onto the bed.

We were two bodies who had been without love for so long. We wanted each other. We needed each other. So desperately, that sex was quick and the release short. It made us hungry for more.

So we made love again. Slowly, sensual, savouring.

The fire within us smouldered. It burned. It exploded.

I screamed with the lightning strike of orgasm. Sparks cascaded through me, lighting up every nerve ending I had.

I was alive. After witnessing so much death, my body finally understood what it meant to live.

Chapter Thirty Five

LAY IN BED listening to Stephen's heavy breathing as he slept beside me.

The bedclothes were draped across my waist, leaving my top half and my feet exposed to the air. I had fallen asleep like that because my body had been hot and sweaty, but now I was starting to feel cold. I could have covered myself up again, but I didn't want to risk dozing off. I needed to get back to the control room to help Freddi. I was only supposed to be going to my room to get changed.

I stepped over various bits of crumpled and discarded clothing to reach the wardrobe.

Before I reached it, I saw the P-tab sitting on the side where I had left it.

I picked it up and looked at its blank screen. I gave it a shake, but it didn't do anything.

My mission to get dressed forgotten, I sat back down on the bed and remembered the last message I had read on it. It almost didn't seem real. I fiddled with the device in the hope of bringing it back to life so I could read the DNA report again.

Stephen stirred.

He moaned with the deep tones of a man's waking yawn. "Morning," he said. "Is it morning?"

I had no idea. In space, there is no day and night. Only the ones which we invent for ourselves. "It could be morning back in Londos, I don't know."

He pulled himself up to sitting and draped his arms around me. He was strong and comforting, but also heavy and sweaty from the aftermath of sex.

"What are you doing?" he said.

"Trying to get my P-tab to work."

"I couldn't get mine to work earlier, either. I think the computer purge must have been triggered back on the research station."

"I thought that was supposed to be targeted on the document," I said.

"It was. But my P-tab went blank in the middle of me using it, like turning it on had initiated some sort of deletion sequence. Does it matter?"

"There was something on here that I wanted to read again. I was going to show you."

I wriggled out from under his arms and crawled up to the top of the bed. I sat with my back against the wall and covered my nakedness with the top sheet. Stephen pulled the pillow out from under his head and used it to cushion his back while he sat up beside me.

"What were you going to show me?" he asked.

I sighed. This was a conversation I had not had time to rehearse. "You know you said it was impossible for King John to be my father?"

"I remember. I thought you believed me."

"I did, but I wanted to be sure. Which was why I got the scientists on the station to run a DNA test."

He raised his eyebrows. "A DNA test?"

"You left behind one of your hairs after the funeral. My mother had a box with some clothes she was making for King John. They used both of them to compare with a sample of my DNA."

"And it confirmed what I told you," said Stephen. "King John is not your father. We are not related, Cassy, it's impossible. I told you."

"Yes, but they also ran a test that I wasn't expecting. They ran a paternity test comparing King John's DNA to yours. It was negative. They found a familial match, but not a paternal match. I thought it might be a mistake, but if the first test was right, how could the second test be wrong?"

He turned away from me. Took a breath. Like he was working out what to say. "I suppose if I denied it, you would only root around until you found out everything."

"It's true?" I said.

"It seems you have uncovered one of the Regellan family secrets."

"I didn't mean to. I only wanted to know if my mother had been King John's mistress, I swear."

"It is still possible they were having an affair," said Stephen. "Your mother's husband was dead, John was in a loveless marriage to my mother – their sexual relations were few and far between, if you believe court gossip. Which, knowing my mother, I do.

It was a marriage of political convenience, as I think everyone knows."

"Yes," I said.

"What they managed to keep out of the court gossip, was that King John couldn't father children. He had been very sick with the plague before he married my mother: it had not only weakened his lungs, it had destroyed his fertility. But he was the only male heir in the Aberchan line and my mother was determined to press ahead to secure an alliance of the two ruling families. She believed children were necessary to cement that alliance and ensure a succession, so she arranged a sperm donation from John's elderly father. The man had never been sick with the plague and was fertile despite his years. So my mother married, John became King, and she was rewarded with two successful pregnancies: first the twins, my two older brothers Richard and James; and then me. Which is why all three of us have traits from my father's side of the family, even though John is not my biological father."

I let the information sink in. "Wow."

"But, as I say, it's a family secret. I would appreciate it if the knowledge doesn't go beyond this room."

Chapter Thirty Six

Ship didn't respond to me when I asked her how long I had been in my room, but the clock on my screen said it had been more than three hours.

Three hours.

I was only supposed to have gone to my room for a change of clothes.

Getting dressed and tying my hair up into an untidy ball, I headed for the door. Stephen asked for me to wait so he could come with me, but I didn't want to make our tryst appear even more obvious than it already was and so I asked him to follow me after a few minutes. I hurried into the corridor and then broke into a run, not as if getting there a few seconds quicker would make any difference.

When I reached the control room, Freddi turned to stop me at the entrance. I was going to apologise for not being there sooner and say I had fallen asleep, but his expression suggested he had something else on his mind.

"Don't come in just yet," he said.

"What's going on?"

Inside, standing at one of the consoles, was Keya.

"Give her a minute," said Freddi, his voice soft and quiet.

"What's she doing?"

"The Fertillan Guard ship sent over a list of survivors they rescued from the debris."

I understood. She had to be reading the names. Every one of them was a person she knew. Every name not on the list was a person who was probably dead.

I waited and listened to my own breathing as it slowed after the run. Keya made no sound. She just stood at the console, looking at the screen.

At last, she turned away from it. She leant back on the console and faced us with streaks of silent tears visible on her cheeks. "Twenty-two names," she said, holding back the emotion. "Out of 147 people."

Freddi and I stepped further inside.

"I'm sorry, Keya," I said.

"How am I going to tell their families?"

"The rescuers will find more survivors," Freddi assured her.

She shook her head. "No. It's nearly five hours since the station was destroyed. *Five hours.* If any pods are left out there, the people inside them will be gasping their last oxygen. They'll suffocate inside a ball barely big enough for their own bodies. It would have been better if they had been torn apart in the explosion. At least it would have been quick."

Stephen walked in behind us. His footsteps sounding loud as his military boots struck the floor.

"Has something happened?" he said.

Keya saw him and the emotion she had been holding back exploded in a torrent of rage. *"You!"* she screamed. Her fists clenched. Anger reddened her face. She walked up to him and looked him in the eye. *"You killer! You murderer!"*

The fury in her words sent spit out of her mouth and onto his cheek. Stephen didn't let it rile him. "I didn't destroy your station," he said.

"Liar!"

"I came only to recover stolen property."

"You came with your death squad and you rounded up every person and then you *killed* them. Like the murdering bastard you are."

She launched herself at him. *"My staff!"* Pushed him. *"My friends!"* Beat him with her fists. *"My lover!"*

Stephen stepped backwards from the assault, even though his bigger and stronger body could have easily fought her off. Freddi and I grabbed Keya and pulled her away from him. She screamed and cried and kicked and the two of us were only just about strong enough to contain her and bring her to the floor.

Beneath all the screaming, I thought I heard my name.

It wasn't Freddi who said it. He was trying to calm Keya. "This is not the way, Keya. Do you hear me? Not the way."

Then I heard it again. Spoken timidly by a female voice.

"Quiet!" I shouted.

"For the Deity's sake," said Freddi. "Let her scream all she likes."

"No, I think I heard the ship."

I tried to listen, but Keya's screams had turned into loud sobbing. "Everybody quiet!"

As her sobs became crying, the ship spoke again, and this time I heard her for sure. "Cassy?"

"Yes, Ship?" I said, looking up at her speakers.

"I don't want to die, Cassy."

"No one else is going to die, Ship."

I looked at Freddi and saw my concern reflected in his face.

"But the man…" said Ship. "He won't let me say the thing I want to say. I'm scared, Cassy."

I jumped to my console and ran a scan. There, on the readout, marked by a red dot flashing in the engine room on the schematics of the ship, was a life sign that shouldn't have been there.

"We've got an intruder," I said. "In the engine room. He must have got into Ship's systems."

Freddi stood. "I'll fetch an EEW and get down there."

He ran out of the control room. I abandoned my console and ran after him.

I CLUTCHED THE EEW with both hands as I edged towards the engine room. The weapon was a small handgun, a spare, and not as familiar as the one that had been shot out of my hand on the research station. But it was enough to confront an unarmed intruder. If he or she was, in fact, unarmed.

As I neared, I felt the pulsating energy of the engines get stronger. They were on slow burn, keeping systems ticking over, but even so their power reverberated through the fabric of that part of the ship. They were the chambers of a heart that kept us flying through space, and could only be accessed via the engine room. A room which also contained the brain that controlled everything: the computer we called Ship.

Freddi joined me at my side. He, too, held a small EE handgun.

"How the vac did someone get in here without us knowing?" Freddi whispered.

"It must have been while we were on the station," I replied.

"Let's hope to the Deity that it's just some scared scientist who got lost."

"Yeah," I said, not believing for a second that was who it could be.

We advanced to where I expected to use my palm print to open the blast door. But the thick, heavy panel was already open enough for a slim person to pass through. By the side of it was the charred remains of the lockpad. A casualty, it appeared, of EE fire. I looked to Freddi to check he had seen it too. By his shocked expression, I saw that he had. Whoever had done this was no lost scientist.

I leant against the wall and took off my boots so I could slip inside quietly on the pads of my feet. Freddi grabbed my sleeve and shook his head to suggest that I shouldn't go in there. But one of us had to and I was more agile than him. Besides, I was the captain.

Holding my breath, my gun ready to fire, I padded through the gap between the door and its frame.

Leading with my gun, I peered inside. The engine room appeared normal. The intruder was nowhere to be seen and the bank of lights on the left wall were all shining dots of green to indicate the engines behind them were working normally. To the right of centre, a workstation which gave direct access to the ship's computer systems, curved round like a flight console and appeared untouched and unmanned.

I crept in further. Freddi padded in behind me.

"Cassy!" said Ship suddenly out of the speakers above. "You're here!"

"Drakh," I said under my breath as any cover we had was blown.

I saw the EE blast shoot past us before I saw the man who fired it. Energy struck the door, sending sparks in all directions as Freddi and I leapt out of the way. I shot off a blast of my own and it struck the console, causing a man in Fertillan Guard uniform to duck back behind it.

I suddenly realised there was only one place that had cover in the engine room, and he – whoever he was – was standing behind it. I rushed back to the door, but another blast seared across my path and sent me staggering backwards.

At the console, the man in brown had the barrel of his EE rifle pointing straight at me. "Move again and I'll kill you."

I saw his face clearly then: it was Trevel.

I lifted my EEW, but before I could take aim, he fired. Energy cut through the air, sizzling past my ear, and struck Freddi in the arm. He screamed as it burned into the flesh of his forearm and he sunk to his knees with the pain. He dropped his weapon to the floor as the smell of burnt skin and blood rose into the air.

"Do you really want to try to shoot me, Individual Sesaan Cassandra?" said Trevel over the sound of Freddi's agonised cries. "There are two of you and one of me, but you are the ones exposed and I am not. Also, I have military training whereas you two, I believe, are a seamstress's daughter and a farmer. Who do you think has the better chance?"

I trembled as I held my gun. I didn't want to relinquish it – my only defence – but I didn't want to be shot either.

"Drop your weapon," Trevel demanded. "And kick it out in front of you."

I hesitated.

Ship's voice came over the speakers. "I don't want you to die, Cassy. I don't want *me* to die."

"It's okay, Ship," I said, as I let my arm go limp and allowed the gun to slip from my fingers. It clattered to the floor and I kicked it away.

"Now come and sit in front of me," said Trevel, motioning with his rifle towards the engine panel. "Where I can keep an eye on you. Both of you."

I helped Freddi to his feet and looked at his wound as we both went where we were told. A slice of flesh the width of a rifle blast had been burnt off of his forearm. He was lucky his arm hadn't been completely severed. It was bleeding a bit, but the energy had done much to cauterise the wound and he was unlikely to die from it. If we managed to live that long.

Trevel trained his rifle on us every step of the way. "Of course, I could just kill you now and be rid of you."

My heart screamed with desperation as I remembered what he had done to the woman pirate in our control room. He said he would let her live and then blew out her brains.

I helped Freddi sit down and I sat beside him. I looked at the barrel of Trevel's rifle and hoped our lives were more valuable to him than that of a pirate.

A voice called out from behind the door. "Don't kill them, Trevel."

It was Stephen.

"Sire?" said Trevel, as incomprehension rippled across his face.

"It's Marshal Commander Regellan," called Stephen's voice. "I'm unarmed. I'm coming in."

I heard the sound of Stephen's boots before I saw his raised hands emerge through the blast door, followed by the rest of him stepping gingerly inside.

Trevel kept the rifle trained on us as he stared, disbelieving, at his commanding officer.

"Sire," he said. "What are you doing here? You should have gone back to our ship."

"Put the rifle down, Trevel."

Stephen took two more steps forward; the green of the indicator lights casting a glow on his face as he got closer to the engine panel. Trevel kept his rifle trained on us.

"I *order* you to put it down."

"I can't, Sire. The code must be destroyed."

"What code?" said Stephen. "There is no code here."

"This ship was the conduit. There could be a copy on board. The knowledge cannot be allowed to survive."

"*I* am your commanding officer! You will put down that rifle and surrender to *me*."

The green glow on Stephen's face started to turn yellowy orange. I looked behind me to see the green lights were blinking out and being replaced by red.

"With respect, Commander, I do not follow your orders on this matter."

Stephen took another couple of steps towards us. He was almost in a position to become our human shield, but not yet. "Whose orders do you follow?"

Trevel ignored the question. "The code must be destroyed," he repeated.

"Did you purge the computer devices on the research station against my express order? Is that what happened to our P-tabs?"

I could tell he was playing for time. And if I, the daughter of a seamstress could sense it, then it was almost certain a military man like Trevel could too.

I looked across at where I had kicked my EEW over by the door. I doubted Stephen could distract Trevel long enough for me to reach it. But I needed to be ready if I got the chance, and I rehearsed the necessary moves in my head.

"I'm sorry, Sire," said Trevel. "It was necessary."

"What about blowing up the research station. Was that necessary too?"

"The scientists had the document. They had read it. The knowledge must be destroyed."

The rumble of the engines increased.

Ship cried out from her speakers. "Cassy, I don't want to die!"

Stephen glared at Trevel. "Trevel, what are you doing?"

"The computer's defences were more sophisticated than I expected, it took me a long time to break through them. I thought I would wipe it clean and that would be an end to it, but the lead scientist from the research station is here. I'm sorry, Sire, I thought you would have returned to our ship by now."

The room shook. Even at full power, the engines wouldn't normally do that.

"He's going to blow us up!" said Freddi.

"Trevel!" shouted Stephen. "Stop this now. If you blow up this ship, it'll kill me – you'll be committing treason of the highest order."

"I'm sorry, S–"

An energy blast ripped through the room and struck Trevel in the side of the head. It burnt into his skull and splattered brain out the other side. His lifeless body flopped to the floor.

We all looked towards the origin of the blast.

Keya stood just inside the door. The hilt of my EEW was clasped in her trembling hands as she pointed it at the spot where Trevel had been.

"Bastard," she said.

Freddi scrambled to his feet. Running on the increasingly shaky floor – holding his wounded arm at his chest – he stepped over Trevel's dead body to the workstation.

"Ship?" I called out. "We need to stop the engines. Can you do that?"

"I can't, Cassy. The man… did things. I wanted to tell you, Cassy, but the man…"

I shook my head. She was going to be of no help to us.

"We're going to have to do this manually," shouted Freddi from behind the workstation. He had his head down and his one good hand was rapidly moving all over the controls. "Cassy, at the bottom of the engine panel, there should be a series of access points marked 'engines A, B and C.'"

I turned to the panel and looked down. I saw exactly what he described: a black, rectangular plate with white lettering which said '*Engine A*'. "Got it!"

"Flip it down from the top – it's hinged at the bottom – and you should see two buttons."

The plate was stiff from hardly ever being opened, but it flipped down with a bit of force. The two buttons were inset on either side of words written in red: '*emergency engine shutdown*'. "What next?"

"Press both of them simultaneously and keep them pressed down until all the lights above go green. Do it for all three engines."

I pushed at the buttons and stared up at the red lights as my body shook and the engines burned with fury.

Stephen and Keya ran over and pulled at the other plates to reveal the emergency shutdown buttons for engines B and C.

"The engine overload was triggered by the computer," said Freddi. "I'm going to have to shut it down."

The first red light turned to green above me. I kept pushing. Beside me, Stephen and Keya pushed at their buttons. We exchanged hopeful and terrified glances.

More lights turned green. Blinking one by one at first, and then in twos and threes until a cascade of green obliterated the red and the shaking lessened.

The rumble of the engines lowered in pitch, like they were sighing, as the power dissipated within them.

As the room calmed, Ship's desperate cry called out, "Cassy! I don't want to die! I don't want to…"

I looked across at where Freddi stood at the workstation. He stopped operating the controls as her voice faded to nothing.

He leant – almost collapsed – against the wall behind him as he clutched his wounded arm and looked up to the ceiling. "I'm sorry, Ship," he said. "I had to destroy you to stop you destroying us."

All the lights were green.

The engines fell silent.

I let go of the buttons and sank to the floor.

Chapter Thirty Seven

WE STOOD IN the shuttle bay: Freddi, Stephen, Keya and myself.

In front of us was the second-hand shuttle that had added so much to our repair bill. Its hull had the carbon scorch marks of space debris it had encountered in an earlier life and there were a few dents in the outside, but pre-flight checks had confirmed it was perfectly serviceable.

Like us.

Freddi clutched his bandaged arm to his chest, but he was confident he would regain full use of it. Keya had lost so much, but still had her surviving staff to return to. Stephen was to resume command of the Fertillan Guard and get back to the royal household. While I – battered, exhausted and confused – was still the freelance captain of my own spaceship.

I looked at Keya. There was a numbness to her now. Brought on by grief, or possibly acceptance, it was hard to know.

"Are you sure you want to go to the Fertillan Guard ship?" I asked her.

She nodded. "My surviving staff are there."

"You're not going to kill him on the journey?" said Freddi, nodding across to Stephen.

"There's been enough killing," she said.

"And you," said Stephen to Freddi. "Are you sure you don't want me to send across one of my engineers to take a look at your ship computer?"

Freddi shook his head. "I wiped the whole thing and returned it to factory settings. Whatever Trevel did to it, it's gone now. It will take some tinkering, but I'll get the ship running again."

Then Stephen turned to me. "Cassy," he said.

I didn't know what to feel because I felt everything all at once: sadness, yearning, love, desire, fear and uncertainty. I had to bypass my feelings to speak and so I uttered something practical. "Don't forget to send the shuttle back on a return trajectory."

"Of course," he said.

We looked at each other in a shared moment of indecision.

Then he stepped forward and kissed me. A lover's kiss that drew me in and stirred the fire within me. A kiss that lasted long and disconnected us from everything else. There was no Freddi and Keya, there was no shuttle and no shuttle bay. There were only his lips and my lips, his passion and my passion, our need to be together and our need to be apart.

All too soon, he stepped away and took his kiss with him. But he left the taste of it and the fire it had ignited.

"Goodbye, Cassy," said Stephen. He turned and walked across to the shuttle.

Keya said her farewells and joined him.

I watched them walk up the steps into the hatch until Freddi reminded me that we had to clear the area ready for the atmosphere to be sucked back into the rest of the ship and the shuttle to depart.

As we left, Freddi asked me a question I couldn't answer. "What's going on with you and the prince?"

"I don't know," I said. "He's a complicated man."

"The way he kisses you tells me that he likes you."

"I like him," I confessed. "But I despise the Fertillan Guard and I'm out of place in the royal household. How can a freelance spaceship captain be with a prince?"

"Looks like I'm stuck with you for a bit longer, then," said Freddi.

"I hope that's not a bad thing."

"No, Cassy," he said. "It's not a bad thing at all."

* * *

ALSO BY JANE KILLICK...

Perceivers

Mind Secrets

Mind Control

Mind Evolution

Mind Power

Echoes (coming in 2020)

Echoes of Death

Echoes of Betrayal

Echoes of Tomorrow

Echoes of Yesterday

Sign up to my newsletter to receive updates on all my latest releases:

janekillick.com/newsletter